The Velvet Spy

THE WW1 JOURNALS OF GINGER GOLD
BOOK ONE

LEE STRAUSS

la
plume

The Velvet Spy ~ Volume 1

Copyright © 2025 by Lee Strauss

Cover by Jordan Strauss

Library and Archives Canada Cataloguing in Publication

Title: The Velvet Spy / Lee Strauss.

Names: Strauss, Lee (Novelist), author.

Description: Series statement: The war time journal of Lady Gold ; volume 1

Identifiers: Canadiana (print) 20250162733 | Canadiana (ebook) 20250162741 | ISBN 9781774095300 (softcover) | ISBN 9781774095331 (IngramSpark softcover) | ISBN 9781774095348 (Bookvault softcover) | ISBN 9781774095317 (Kindle) | ISBN 9781774095324 (EPUB) | ISBN: 978-1-77409-550-8 (softcover)

Subjects: LCGFT: Spy fiction. | LCGFT: Novels.

Classification: LCC PS8637.T739 V45 2025 | DDC C813/.6—dc23

Chapter One

HAPPY BIRTHDAY TO ME!

July 31st, 1912

HOW FABULOUS THAT I found this journal today, tucked away at the bottom of my wardrobe! Good old Pippins—our English butler in London—gave it to me years ago as a parting gift when Father whisked me off to America so he could marry Sally. Pips said it was for me to record my new adventures.

I'm ashamed to admit I didn't pen a single word until today. I think I was simply too sad back then. But no matter— I'm writing now, and this will be the first of many entries, I hope. I imagine myself as an old woman, sitting by the fire, thumbing through these pages as they bring back cherished memories of a long and adventure-filled life.

This old leather-bound journal takes me right back to that emotional time. I cried enough tears to fill an ocean and remember telling Father, dramatically, that I would surely cause a flood to rival Noah's. At eight years old, I was well-versed in my biblical studies, though in hindsight, I might have bordered on heresy with my little tantrum.

The first week of my so-called "adventure" was spent aboard a big steamship, feeling wretchedly sick to my stomach the whole way. There were far too many embarrassing episodes involving a bucket and Father holding back my long hair so I wouldn't soil it with vomit. I was convinced I was being punished for some unknown offense.

Hartigan House—though large and sometimes lonely—was my home. And Pips, dear Pips, was my good friend. He often entertained me with games of I Spy or Noughts and Crosses.

"Very good, Little Miss," he'd say with a twinkle in his blue eyes when I won, which I did often. Looking back, I suspect Pips wasn't above letting me win, even when I hadn't earned it.

Father claimed he'd uprooted us because I needed a mother, though I think he simply wanted a wife. Sally—a woman half his age—turned out to be a sufficient spouse in the end, but I could never bring myself to call her "Mother."

Well, Pips, you'd be glad to know things turned out all right here in America. My childhood was pleasant—school, new friends, and learning to ride horses and shoot guns, a pastime that's very popular here, even beyond the elite. I went to an excellent school, and I focused on studying modern languages and science. Boston is a beautiful city, and much of it reminds me of England.

Oh, and I suppose I should mention that Father and Sally produced a sister for me—Louisa. She's dark-haired, with a sweet teardrop-shaped face, and the very image of Sally. I don't hold that against her, though. She's as spoiled as they come, with Sally pandering to her every whim and Father far less strict with her than he ever was with me. With ten years between us, we don't have much in common, but I adore her all the same.

This afternoon was spent preparing for the evening's activities. Father was hosting a soirée in honor of my nineteenth birthday, and I planned to enjoy a large slice of Mrs. Bakker's Dutch Dark Chocolate Cake. Her cakes are legendary—so rich and moist they melt in your mouth like cocoa-laced ecstasy. My mouth waters just thinking about them.

Father adores throwing soirées—or as in this case, "dinner parties," as the Americans call them. I often feel caught between two cultures. Outside this Beacon Hill brownstone, I'm American, but inside, I cling to my English roots. Father and I still enjoy traditional tea with scones and clotted cream, served properly, the English way. Our conversations often turn to politics—both here and across the Atlantic. Some of the news is deeply worrisome, but I won't dwell on that tonight.

"Not too tight," I told my maid Molly as she tightened the straps on my corset. The columnar corset forced me to stand straight and tall, though I silently thanked the heavens that those horrid S-bend corsets had gone out of fashion. It's a wonder we aren't all deformed!

Molly helped me into a gown of shiny emerald silk, with an open neckline and slender sleeves that ended at my elbows. I spun in front of the long mirror, admiring the fitted gown with its beautifully contrasting lace ruffle.

"The color brings out your eyes, Miss Hartigan," Molly said as she pinned my red hair into an elegant coiffure, a delicate wreath of ribbon encircling the style.

Molly held up a hand mirror. "You'll be the belle of the ball, miss."

"Thank you, Molly," I said, smiling. "I'm excited for the evening, though I do wish Father hadn't assigned me a date."

An English gentleman would be joining the festivities, he'd announced. Apparently, the gentleman is the son of a family friend—a baron, no less. I worry my American friends might find his title pompous. No matter. After tonight, I doubt I'll see him again.

What did Father say his name was? Right—Daniel, Lord Gold.

Chapter Two

THE INTRODUCTION OF LORD GOLD

August 1, 1912

UNBELIEVABLE! Father used my birthday party to set me up. While I thought he merely wanted me to have an escort for the soirée, the truth came out in the end—he invited Lord Gold to Boston with the intention that I should marry him!

The evening started well enough. The drawing room of our Boston brownstone isn't nearly as grand as the one at Hartigan House in London, but it suited the size of the party. (As a side note, our brownstone isn't distinguished enough to have a name and is referred to simply as "our house" or "our home" or, more specifically, "6685 Beacon Street.")

In attendance were Father, Sally, and Louisa, of course; Daniel Lord Gold; my dear friend Elizabeth Squire with her brother John; several of my school friends; and Father's business partner and his wife. Mrs. Bakker outdid herself with a marvelous three-course meal of codfish in lemon sauce, glazed duck with roasted carrots, beets, caramelized onions, and a fresh salad dressed in oil and vinegar, followed, of course by the amazing chocolate cake. We washed it down with glasses of the finest California wines—the growing temperance movement would have been horrified!

Glasses were raised in my honor. Father toasted: "To my lovely daughter—intelligent, capable, and highly eligible."

Everyone laughed as they toasted me. Father winked. At first, I thought he was winking at me, but then I realized it was directed at Lord Gold! Lord Gold's lips twitched ever so slightly, and the nuance made my stomach twist. What was my father up to!

Dinner was followed by dancing in the drawing room. Father had hired a small band that played favorites such as "That Haunting Melody" and "Moonlight Bay."

To spite my father, I immediately suggested to John Squire that he ask me to dance before Lord Gold could claim me.

"You look ravishing, Miss Hartigan," John said as he guided me around the room.

"Why, thank you, Mr. Squire."

I made a point of staring defiantly at Father as we passed him. George Hartigan is a man accustomed to getting his way, but he simply lit his pipe and let smoke billow from his nose.

Of course, I couldn't avoid Lord Gold all evening. Sure enough, after the third song, he approached and requested my hand.

His grip on me was acceptably loose yet confident. Though not handsome at first glance, he does have pleasant blue eyes, well-trimmed honey-blond hair, and a tailored suit of the highest quality. The tails of his jacket fell perfectly over his pressed trousers, and a black bow tie rested neatly at the neck of his starched white shirt.

He gazed down at me with a glint of amusement.

"I feel I have offended you, Miss Hartigan," he said.

"I don't care to be the object of someone else's mirth, Lord Gold."

"If you're suggesting I've been anything but gentlemanly, I must beg your pardon."

"Your manners are not in question. It's your motive."

Lord Daniel spun me around the room, his dancing undeniably skilled. I admit I was momentarily distracted by his cologne.

"You are rather perceptive, Miss Hartigan," he said eventually.

"I like to think so. Are you here to visit my father, or is there more?"

"We are negotiating, you could say. It's a conversation best left for tomorrow. Your father has a meeting planned."

"If I am involved in the negotiations in any way, shouldn't I be included?"

Lord Gold tightened his hold slightly. "I certainly hope so."

The nerve! How dare he insinuate...

The band began to play "Turn Off Your Light, Mr. Moon-Man," and I felt my cheeks burn at the lyrics. Even now, the tune plays in my head:

"When the Moon is shining yellow
And a girl is with her fellow
Both are getting nice and mellow..."

"I quite like this song," Lord Gold remarked, clearly amused.

"I'm sure you do, Lord Gold." I pulled back and fixed him with a direct look. "I'm an educated woman, and, as you've noted, perceptive. Are you and my father negotiating terms for my hand in marriage?"

Lord Gold grinned crookedly, a dimple appearing on his cheek. I suddenly had the distinct feeling that my father wasn't the only man in the room used to getting his way.

7

"Would it be so awful if we were?"

"If you think I would marry a man I didn't know or didn't choose for myself, you are sorely mistaken."

"Then I suppose you'll have to get to know me, Miss Hartigan." He smiled slyly. "In time, I hope you'll choose me yourself."

Blast him!

It all became clearer this morning. My Father had the decency to invite me to the meeting regarding my so-called future. I don't think I've ever been so angry with him in my life. Why did he have to spring this on me?

The meeting was held in Father's study. Paneled with rich, dark wood, it contains his large desk, a wall of shelves, and a fireplace unused during the summer. The room always smells faintly of his pipe tobacco, reminiscent of his study at Hartigan House.

Lord Gold and I sat in the chairs facing Father's desk. I wore a day dress of lavender satin and lace, determined to look my best. I needed every ounce of confidence to go up against two determined men.

Father lit his pipe, his hand trembling slightly. I frowned. "Are you all right, Father? You seem a little shaky."

He laughed it off. "Perhaps I'm a bit nervous."

As he should be! I folded my arms. "Let's get on with it, shall we?" I turned to Lord Gold. "What's in it for you, Lord Gold?"

"Please, call me Daniel."

"Very well. You may call me Georgia." Only those in my intimate circle were permitted to call me Ginger, the nickname bestowed on me by my mother. Daniel was not one amongst them.

"Splendid, Georgia. To answer your question—money."

I huffed. "What a surprise." I turned to Father. "And what's in it for you?"

"Ginger, love," he said, placing his pipe in the ashtray. "You must know I want the very best for you."

"An arranged marriage to a man after your money is the best you can do?"

Father sighed, running a hand over his balding head. "Please, hear me out."

And so I listened, though I can't say I was entirely convinced.

Chapter Three

BOSTON PUBLIC GARDEN

August 3, 1912

I INSISTED on a couple of days to consider the proposition my father and Daniel set forth. I've spent most of the time in a daze, and I think it might help if I set out a list of pros and cons:

PROS
- Married
- Father happy
- Social advantages
- Children will be British

CONS
- Married
- Ginger happy?
- Live in England?
- Abandon any of my vocational pursuits

I'm divided. I've always been a devoted daughter and have wanted to please my father. I believe this need grew stronger after Sally came into our lives. The child in me has always felt in competition with her. For some reason, a union with Daniel is important to Father. It can't just be about a title. Is this his way of ensuring I return to my English roots? Does he feel guilty for taking me away?

Father has often warned me not to lose my British identity, though he always said it with a smile. "One American daughter is enough," he jokes.

Still, I decided to keep an open mind. Father wouldn't force me into anything I don't want to do. The least I could do was be a good hostess to our guest. Daniel has come a long way, after all. I hoped he hadn't spent the journey across the Atlantic hugging a bucket as I had all those years ago.

Father agreed to let Daniel and me walk through the Boston Public Garden unchaperoned.

"Not much can go wrong with a walk across the street," he said. He checked his watch, and I noticed again the slight tremble in his hand. "Please be back in an hour for luncheon."

Daniel nodded. "Of course, sir."

The summer sun was warm, and I chose my white cotton day dress to combat the heat. It's delicately trimmed with lace along the boot-length hem and décolletage. A daring rectangle of white skin is exposed at the neckline. A ruby-red silk ribbon tied around my waist adds a feminine touch, creating an appealing hourglass effect.

I wore my wide-brimmed white straw hat with the large black feather, and I carried a parasol for extra protection from the sun's rays.

Daniel ensured the road was clear of carriages and pedestrians before leading me across the street. We joined other couples and families enjoying the park on this pleasant summer morning.

"It's not London, but I understand the attraction," Daniel said.

I twirled my parasol. "I remember London. But Boston is my home now."

Daniel ducked to meet my gaze. "Do you think you'll ever go back?"

I studied him. The question was loaded. I tilted my head and smiled. "I don't know."

"The lure of the American dream," he said. "Boston is a beautiful city. I think I might like to stay here."

I glanced at him, curious. Was he saying we'd remain in Boston if I agreed to marry him? I supposed I should have asked directly, but I wasn't ready to bring up the subject again so soon.

"Tell me about your life in London," I said.

"Well, actually, I spend most of my time in Hertfordshire, north of London, in our family home."

"Bray Manor," I added, remembering what Father had said.

"Indeed. It's a large, charming old place set amidst wide lawns, and there is a rather enormous pond. Only my sister, my grandmother, and I reside there now, aside from the servants of course."

"Are you close to your sister?"

"Felicia is only ten years old."

"Oh? Just one year older than Louisa. I do hope she has better manners."

Daniel shrugged. "Felicia can be a handful. She's been without a mother since she was an infant, but my grandmother does her best to fill the role."

"Father mentioned that your parents had passed away. I'm so sorry."

"There have been some difficult years."

Despite my best efforts, I felt sympathetic to Daniel's cause. He was only doing what he must to help his family. I couldn't really fault him for that. Even if he was after the Hartigan money, he did at least seem to like me.

"Before..." Daniel waved a hand. "This proposal. Did you have any plans?"

"I've only just completed my education. I'm still weighing my options. Perhaps open my own business."

"Really? How ambitious."

I slowed to a stop and scowled. "You mean for a woman."

Daniel appeared flustered. "No, no, well, yes, I suppose. It's not that I don't think you could do it. You seem to be the kind of lady who's capable of many things. It's just that not many women do."

I appreciated his honesty.

"So you see," I said, continuing to stroll, "marriage at this time in my life would be inconvenient."

"Because you feel you'd have to abandon your plans?"

"It's a social construct of the times.."

Two young boys in knickerbockers and newsboy caps ran toward us, shoving their way between us instead of circling. I yelped.

"Shall I chase them down?" Daniel smirked, smacking his palm playfully with his fist. "I could show those rascals a thing or two about respect."

My indignation slipped away, replaced by amusement at my companion.

"No need to cause a scene, Lord Gold," I said with a giggle. "I wouldn't want the authorities to ship you away before your time."

His dark brow arched. "Before September 29th?"

Michaelmas.

I swallowed and glanced away.

"What if I said you could keep working after we were wed for as long as you liked?"

"That's very radical of you, Daniel."

He grinned. "I believe we are kindred in that regard."

It pleased me that he thought so. "And when the children come?" I asked, forcing myself not to think of what would have to happen between us to produce children.

"The children would have a nurse."

"You're very accommodating, Lord Gold."

He smiled, his eyes twinkling. "I'm starting to feel that marriage to you would be more than a simple arrangement. Not only are you much prettier than I'd imagined, but you're intelligent and strong in spirit." His grin widened. "I'm attracted to you, Georgia Hartigan."

I was stunned and, once again, left without words. I walked on, maddened by the fact that I could feel myself blushing.

Chapter Four

TROUBLE AT QUINCY MARKET

August 8, 1912

DANIEL, Lord Gold, has taken to spending a portion of each day visiting 6685 Beacon Street. I was amused, Father was hopeful, Sally was annoyed—"Is he to be with us every day? He might as well move in—" and little Louisa was utterly enamored.

Louisa, dressed in a pinafore and ribbons, her dark hair curled into ringlets, tugged on Father's smoking jacket. She was the very picture of sweetness. "Is Lord Gold going to come over again today?"

"Yes, love," Father replied jovially.

Louisa hopped up and down, her ringlets bouncing. "Yay!"

Father winked at me. "Somehow the wrong daughter has been caught in the web of Lord Gold's charms."

I laughed. "I do believe you've grown soft on our guest, Louisa."

Even at the tender age of nine, Louisa was quick to take

offense. She didn't like being laughed at and hadn't yet learned the value of laughing at herself.

Her pixie face crumpled into a scowl. "I have not!" She stomped her foot. "Why must you be so nasty, Ginger?" Then, with a huff, she stormed out of the sitting room.

Father shook his head as he pulled out his pipe. "I can only imagine the handful she'll be when she gets older."

"You've had plenty of training with me, Father. I'm sure you'll manage."

He smiled at me with dark, misty eyes. His beard had turned gray seemingly overnight, and the wrinkles around his eyes were more pronounced than I remembered. A sweet sadness gripped my heart. At some point, when I wasn't looking, my father had grown old.

"You were a pleasure, love, and without a mother. Sally spoils that one." He pulled on his pipe and blew out a cloud of smoke. "I'm afraid I'm helpless to stop her."

The doorbell rang, and I heard Grant, our butler, answer it.

I turned to Father. "Lord Gold, I presume?"

Father extinguished his pipe and stood. "I've invited him to take a drive in the carriage into town with us. It's a lovely day, and I thought we could show him the sights."

Grant opened the sitting room doors. "Lord Gold, sir."

Daniel entered, removing his top hat and bowing. I offered a small curtsy, though I felt ruffled and uncertain about how to behave now that I knew Daniel had feelings for me—not just for my father's money.

Sally, informed of Father's plans, presented herself with a flourish. She wore a soft gray lingerie dress with tight lace sleeves, a slender waist, and a long lace hemline. A broad-brimmed hat adorned with rubber fruits and linen flowers perched atop her pile of brunette curls. Though she is in her late thirties, Sally maintains a youthful air. On more than one occasion, she's been mistaken for Father's daughter rather than his wife.

She approached Daniel and lifted a gloved hand for him to kiss. "Lord Gold, it's a pleasure."

Her words belied her private sentiments. She seemed to go out of her way with her appearance and manners, and I briefly wondered if she was attracted to the baron. Though older than Daniel by a good few years, Sally was closer in age to him than to Father. How absurd that both Sally and Louisa had taken an interest in Daniel Gold.

Determined not to let emotions get the better of me, I steeled myself.

Sally turned to me. "Is that what you're wearing?"

She meant to demean me. Though I'd grown inured to such verbal attacks, I wasn't beyond feeling a pinch of embarrassment—especially in front of a guest.

"I've only just learned of the outing," I said, jutting my chin. "Pardon me."

I quickly retreated to my room, where Molly helped me change into a two-piece silk outfit. The cream blouse featured braid and lace trim, and I paired it with a long, pale-blue skirt and jacket.

By the time I rejoined everyone at the entrance, Father had arranged for our carriage to be ready. Father and Sally took the front-facing seat, while Daniel, Louisa, and I sat facing back.

"I want to sit in the middle beside Lord Gold!" Louisa demanded, climbing over my lap. I grunted at her weight—she wasn't a small child anymore. Settling beside Daniel, she stared at him with stars in her eyes. I was grateful for the space between us and made a point of looking the other way.

Father took his role as tour guide seriously.

The Massachusetts State House, with its dome plated in gold leaf, hardly needed pointing out.

"Magnificent," Daniel said.

"It's the seat of the state legislature," Father explained.

We passed Granary Burying Ground.

"The patriots Samuel Adams and Paul Revere are buried there," Father said. "Boston is the seat of American independence."

"We've come a long way since the Revolution," Sally added, her American accent loud and clear.

"I'm starting to feel like the enemy," Daniel said with a grin. "We have a different view of the colonists from my side of the pond."

"Or perhaps Father and I are traitors," I said, exaggerating my English accent to needle Sally.

"Now, now," Father said. "America has been very good to us."

He meant to his pocketbook. The American steel industry was booming.

The streets grew more congested as we neared Quincy Market. At one point, a carriage passed close enough for me to purchase a suffragist newspaper for five cents.

"Please don't fill Louisa's head with those silly ideas," Sally said with a frown. "Men are perfectly suited for running nations. Children need their mothers at home."

"The vote for women wouldn't have to change that," I replied. "It could help many women who aren't as privileged as you and I."

It was a debate we often had.

The cobblestones made for a bumpy ride, and Louisa began to complain.

"Mama, are we there yet? It's hot, and my bottom is starting to hurt."

Daniel grinned at me over the top of her dark head. I couldn't help grinning back.

When we finally reached Faneuil Hall and Quincy Market, I was nearly as irritable as Louisa, though I was careful not to let it show, and eager to stretch my legs.

The market bustled with shoppers and vendors. Daniel paused at a flower stall to purchase a bouquet of roses.

"For you," he said, holding them out. "A peace offering."

"I didn't know we were at war, Lord Gold."

"Oh, but we are, Miss Hartigan," he said with a grin, his dimple showing. "The battleground is your heart."

Oh, mercy!

Before I could respond, Sally's voice cut through the air.

"Louisa! Louisa!"

I ran to her. "Sally?"

"I can't find Louisa!"

I scanned the crowd for my sister's white straw hat and dark ringlets but saw no sign of her.

Father joined us, visibly distressed. "She must be here somewhere."

"I'll find her," Daniel declared. He quickly approached a mounted police officer, gave a description, then spoke with another man and handed him some money. Moments later, Daniel mounted the man's horse and rode off.

Louisa is the epitome of a nuisance, but she is my sister, and I love her. My stomach churned with dread.

I led Father and Sally back to the carriage so we could sit and wait. I fetched lemonade for all of us, but it did little to calm my nerves.

At last, Daniel rode up like a knight in shining armor, with Louisa seated in front of him on the saddle.

Louisa cried many tears of remorse. "I got swept up in the crowd."

Father and Sally thanked Daniel profusely.

"It was my duty and my pleasure," Daniel said humbly. "If you'll excuse me, I have a horse to return."

As he led the mare back to its owner, he glanced over his shoulder and subtly grinned at me.

I can't believe I once thought Daniel Gold wasn't good-looking. I'd never met a more handsome man.

Chapter Five

MEMORIES

August 15, 1912

DANIEL HAS BEEN SUCH a frequent guest at 6685 Beacon Street, spending much time in Father's study, that I'm quite sure they're plotting my future. Surprisingly, I'm not bothered by this fact anymore.

Besides, I won't let myself be coerced into doing anything I don't want to, and Father knows this. I believe Daniel has also become aware of this obstinate character trait of mine.

This morning, Daniel requested that I join him for a walk in the Common. I agreed to a morning stroll, as the humidity in the afternoons at the moment is unbearable—and disastrous for my hair, which takes Molly literally an hour to arrange.

Since Daniel's heroic rescue of Louisa, my little sister has been unabashedly smitten—even more so than before. It would be adorable if she weren't so annoying. Naturally, she made a scene in the sitting room where Daniel waited for me, demanding to come along. Sally, of course, asked me to take her.

"She needs fresh air and exercise."

I wanted to ask why Sally didn't take her out herself, but I refrained, not wanting to sound petty in front of Daniel. "Very well," I agreed reluctantly.

"We'd be pleased to have the company of Miss Louisa," Daniel proclaimed amiably. He held out his arm, and Louisa skipped to him, linking her thin limb through his. She even glanced over her shoulder to stick her tongue out at me. Brat!

The walk turned out to be quite pleasant. I wore a white lacy summer dress with loose sleeves that ended at my elbows, and a lavender sash. A matching ribbon decorated my flat, broad-rimmed hat, which Molly had secured with a dozen hatpins. The ensemble managed the heat well, especially since a breeze whispered through the elms. Louisa, with all the energy of a locomotive, scampered after squirrels and collected pebbles.

I twirled my parasol and glanced up at Daniel. "Tell me more about Bray Manor." Now that I knew him a little better, I found I was quite interested.

Daniel planted his smooth hands in the pockets of his summer suit jacket. "It's a very large house in need of repair, but the grounds are splendid. My grandmother has a beautiful rose garden, and the lake in the park is large enough for taking a rowboat on."

"That does sound nice. Very pastoral."

Daniel grinned, looking rather handsome in his straw boater hat. "It's quiet, I'll give you that."

"Just the three of you in that big place?"

"Well, we do have staff, of course, though not as many as we used to. Quite frankly, not as many as are needed to keep the place up."

Thus, the reason he was here in Boston, courting me. He needed Hartigan money. I decided to let that irritation slide for now. The day was too lovely to let a bee get in my bonnet.

"What's your grandmother like?"

Daniel's brows jumped as a smirk spread over his face. "Ambrosia the Dowager Lady Gold is a force of nature. There isn't a villager in Chesterton who isn't in a quake of her. I don't blame her for her strong personality. She's had to act as the head of the family while I was under age—since both my grandfather and father have been gone for many years—and as a surrogate mother to both me and my little sister. I'm able to fend for myself now, of course, but Felicia is only ten."

"If she's anything like Louisa, then your grandmother has her hands full."

"I'm afraid Felicia does keep my grandmother on her toes. Much like Louisa, she's spirited, with a mind of her own and no inhibitions in sharing it. Grandmother handles her more like a general than a mother, I'm afraid. Firm and demanding. But Felicia is in want of nothing. Grandmother makes sure of that."

I didn't doubt that Lady Gold needed to be a bear to manage such an energetic child, much less run an estate. Sally barely manages half as much responsibility.

"Grandmother even bought a motorcar!" Daniel added with a note of pride. "A 1904 Coventry Humber."

I was amazed. "Does she drive it?"

"No, of course not, we have a man for that. She prefers the carriage, but the purchase certainly caused the village to hold her in high esteem. It's mainly used to take her and Felicia to church on Sunday mornings, to great effect. The King himself would be jealous."

I couldn't help but smile. I haven't met Lady Gold, but I already admire her.

Listening to Daniel talk about his home made me miss London. Which was odd since I haven't been there since I was a child, and my memories are limited. But now, I truly hope to go back someday.

Louisa bounded between us, interrupting our talk. She demanded candy from a street vendor, and our meaningful conversation was over. Next time, I'm not letting her tag along, no matter how much Sally insists.

Chapter Six

FENWAY PARK

August 28, 1912

DANIEL TOOK me to a baseball game at the new Fenway Park today, and what a wonderful time it was. Even now, as I write this, I can't help but smile. I want to capture every detail, so that years from now, I can look back and remember it all.

"It opened just five days after the Titanic sank in the spring," I said as we approached the red-brick facade. "It's supposed to be state of the art—a real 20th-century ballpark."

The entrance was bustling with activity. A billboard for Sterling Ale was displayed the left side, featuring a picture of a covered wagon pulled by a team of horses. A flagpole on the roof pierced the sky, the stars and stripes flapping proudly in the late-summer breeze. The crowd was predominantly men, dressed in dark suits and hats, though I spotted a few families with excited children clutching small pennants. Policemen on horseback patrolled the grounds, their mounts stamping and snorting as the officers surveyed the gathering.

"It's a rather grand place for a game, isn't it?" Daniel remarked and then tipped his straw boater back on his forehead to better be able to gaze up at the grand facade.

After navigating the shuffling crowd, we reached our seats. Daniel had arranged for us to sit in the top row of Section 'E,' just to the right of home plate. The newly painted stands gleamed in the sunlight, the fresh wood scent still faintly detectable beneath the stronger aromas of roasted peanuts and cigars.

The ball diamond was breathtaking, larger than I'd imagined, and perfectly symmetrical with its bright green field and the stark white chalk lines marking the bases. The energy in the stadium was palpable, the chatter and laughter of the thousands of fans—I heard it was over ten thousand!—creating an almost musical hum. Below us stretched a sea of hats, fedoras and bowlers bobbing as men exchanged jokes and predictions.

"I heard that when the Red Sox are on a winning streak, this crowd can almost double in size," I said. "Try to imagine that!"

"Hard to picture," Daniel admitted, gazing out over the crowd. "Boston Red Sox against Chicago White Sox? Rather unimaginative team names, wouldn't you say?"

I grinned. "They're not all named after male hosiery."

Daniel chuckled, the deep, rolling sound sending a pleasant shiver up my spine.

"Sometimes a woman brings proper perspective," I teased.

"This I have found to be true," he replied, tipping the brim of his hat.

A tremendous roar erupted as the Red Sox team jogged onto the field. The crowd rose to their feet in unison, clapping and cheering with an enthusiasm that was impossible not to join.

"That's Smokey Joe Wood," I said, pointing to the tall,

confident pitcher taking his place on the mound. "Boston's ace pitcher. He's only twenty-two years old and already a household name."

"How do you know all this?" Daniel looked at me with an amused expression.

"It's hard to avoid," I said with a shrug. "The stadium's opening and the Red Sox's success are front-page news in every Boston paper. Supporting baseball is fast becoming a part of the city's culture—even for women."

"Righto," Daniel said with a twinkle in his eye. "I'll admit, I prefer cricket if I'm playing. I am, after all, a proper Brit. But as a spectator, the atmosphere of a baseball game is rather invigorating, don't you think?"

As the game began, I found myself swept up in the rhythm of the plays. The crack of the bat was sharp and thrilling, followed by the satisfying thud of the ball hitting the glove or the roar of the crowd as a player dashed toward the bases. One moment that stood out was when Smokey Joe Wood struck out three batters in a row. The crowd erupted into a roar of cheering, hats flying into the air as fans jumped to their feet.

"He's quite good, isn't he?" Daniel said, clapping along with the rest. "I'd wager he's worth his weight in gold to this team."

"And then some," I replied, grinning.

During the seventh inning stretch, a brass band played a lively rendition of "Take Me Out to the Ballgame." Fans waved their hats and sang along, the lyrics echoing through the stadium like an anthem. Vendors wove through the stands, calling out their wares: "Peanuts! Popcorn! Ice-cold drinks!"

Daniel bought us both a 'Fenway Frank,' and we laughed over our efforts to eat without spilling mustard on our clothes. The salty snap of the sausage paired with the soft bun was a delightful treat, and Daniel declared it "a jolly good show" as he polished off the last bite.

The game continued with nail-biting moments—a close double play at second base had the crowd gasping—and when the Red Sox scored their final run, securing a 5-3 victory, the stadium erupted once more. The players jogged off the field, waving to the fans as cheers and applause rained down.

"That was marvelous," Daniel said as the crowd began to thin.

It took ages to exit the stadium, the press of bodies slow-moving but not unpleasant. By the time we strolled through Kenmore Square, the evening air had cooled. Lamplighters appeared with their long poles, igniting the gas lamps one by one, their flames casting a golden glow on the cobblestone streets.

"That was frightfully enjoyable," Daniel said after we walked in companionable silence for a few minutes.

"I agree," I said without hesitation. "Thank you for inviting me. Not a bad move, you know—an Englishman accompanying a Boston woman to a baseball game."

Unable to resist, I batted my eyelashes at him flirtatiously.

Daniel's lips curved into a small smile. After a moment, he offered his arm. "May I?"

I linked my arm through his, smiling as we continued down the cobblestone streets. The soft clinking of the lamplighters' poles and the distant hum of evening life filled the air.

Having Daniel Gold by my side is starting to feel altogether too agreeable.

Chapter Seven

SAYING GOODBYE

September 29, 1912

SOMETIMES THE DAYS you dread the most sneak up on you like thieves. Today was such a day. Michaelmas—the day Daniel, Lord Gold, left for Liverpool.

I was a bundle of nerves, my stomach twisted with emotions I couldn't untangle. Daniel still awaited my answer. So did Father. I was the key to their business deal, a fact I couldn't forget. Yet, this decision had become so much more than just a matter of trade and title.

The clopping of Father's horses echoed off the cobbled streets as the carriage rattled toward the piers. The morning air was cool and crisp, with the tang of autumn in the breeze. But as the harbor came into view, the salty sea air mingled unpleasantly with the disagreeable smell of sewage that Boston Harbor has become infamous for.

"I'm glad to be sailing on a brand-new ship this time," Daniel said, breaking the silence. "The Laconia's maiden voyage was just eight months ago, and she's fitted with 'anti-roll' tanks—the first North Atlantic liner to have them. That should make the journey much more agreeable." His gaze swept across the bustling harbor to the open sea beyond, his expression thoughtful.

"It's a wonder you were able to secure passage at all," Father added. "After that nasty coal workers' strike in England earlier this year."

Small talk filled the carriage as we approached the pier, but the larger conversation—the one that loomed over us—remained unspoken.

The R.M.S. Laconia sat docked, her red-and-black twin stacks towering above the chaotic scene of passengers and porters. Her freshly painted hull gleamed in the sunlight, a sharp contrast to the industrial grime of the surrounding docks. Crowds swarmed the loading pier, clutching bags and luggage cases while Cunard Line officials shouted announcements over the din. Children clung to mothers' skirts, men gestured to porters, and an air of excitement buzzed above the chaos as boarding lines began to form.

Father halted the carriage and climbed out, while our driver unloaded Daniel's luggage. Daniel hired a porter to wheel it toward the ship, and Father extended his hand. "I'll say goodbye now," he said.

The inference was clear: I was meant to walk Daniel to the gangway. This was my moment to give an answer, yet even then, I was undecided. Oh, mercy!

We walked slowly, shoulder to shoulder, the crowd swallowing us. Despite the noise and movement around us, my focus narrowed until Daniel was the only person I saw. His presence seemed to anchor me in the chaos.

He stopped and turned to face me, taking my hands in his. His gaze softened as he ducked slightly to meet my eyes.

"My darling Georgia," he began, his voice steady but tinged with vulnerability. "I'm afraid I can't wait any longer for your answer. I profess to have fallen in love with you, but you know that already. And because I love you, I will accept graciously—albeit sadly—should your answer be no. But if you love me in return, you would make me the happiest of men."

My knees melted, and I nearly swooned. Me, Ginger Hartigan! Daniel's blue eyes brimmed with honesty and kindness. I knew, in the core of my being, that I could trust this man.

I could love this man.

If love was a quickened pulse, the warmth that flooded my cheeks, and the inability to banish thoughts of him from my mind—if love was this deep ache at the thought of being apart—then yes, I did love Daniel.

"Yes," I whispered, my voice dry and barely audible.

His expression brightened. "Yes?"

"Yes! I love you, too." The words felt both terrifying and exhilarating. "I will marry you!"

What happened next is too delicate to record, but I will say that more than one upright citizen huffed with disapproval.

When we came up for air, I laughed, a mix of joy and disbelief spilling out. "I can't believe I'm agreeing to an arranged marriage!"

"Truth be told, neither can I," Daniel said, his smile boyish and endearing. "But I do love you, Georgia, and I can't wait to make you my wife."

Suddenly, the thought of his departure felt unbearable. "Do you really have to go back to England? Can't you stay?"

He sighed, his expression tinged with regret. "I'm afraid I must. There are business and family matters at Bray Manor that require my attention. And I need to spend Christmas with my family. There are just the three of us, and the holidays make a large, mostly empty house like Bray Manor feel all the lonelier."

"Then when will you return?" I asked, my heart sinking at the thought of his absence.

"In the spring," he promised. "Once the winter storms have passed."

Spring. Six months without him stretched before me like an eternity.

"It'll be all right, Georgia," Daniel said gently, as if sensing my dread. "The time will go by quickly, and it will give you plenty of opportunity to plan a beautiful summer wedding."

The ship's horn blasted, a sharp reminder that time had run out. Regret flooded me. I had spent so much of his visit debating our future when I should have been savoring every moment. My blasted pride!

"Oh, Daniel," I said, tears pooling in my eyes. "This will be the longest winter of my life."

"Mine too," he admitted. "But we'll write each other."

"Every day!"

The final boarding call forced him to pull away. He hesitated for just a moment, then kissed my hand and turned, weaving through the crowd toward the gate.

I stood frozen, watching as he ascended the gangway, my heart a tumult of joy and grief. Elation at having found the love of my life warred with the sick ache of saying goodbye. He reached the deck and turned, scanning the crowd until his eyes met mine. He lifted his hat in a final salute, his dimple flashing in a bittersweet smile.

I waved, my arm heavy with the weight of parting, and stayed rooted to the spot until the ship's horn sounded again and the Laconia pulled away from the dock.

The sight of the great ship departing, her stacks trailing smoke into the crisp autumn sky, left an indelible impression.

As the crowd thinned and the chaos of the pier quieted, I made my way back to the carriage where Father waited, his expression unreadable.

"Well?" he asked.

I smiled faintly, though tears streaked my cheeks. "I said yes."

Father's shoulders relaxed, and he reached over to pat my hand. "You've made a good choice, love."

I hoped he was right. But as the Laconia disappeared into the horizon, taking Daniel with her, I realized that while I had found my future, I also faced my greatest test—learning to wait for love.

Chapter Eight

THE MISSING LOCKET

October 15, 1912

"Lord Gold is a fine man, Miss Ginger," Molly said, standing behind me as she worked through the tangles of my hair. "I think you'll be very happy."

I studied her blue-gray eyes in the reflection of the vanity mirror. Father had hired Molly immediately after we arrived in Boston in 1901, and she had been more than a maid—she was a surrogate mother, a confidante, and a steady presence in my life. Over the years, I had learned to read her sincerity, even when her words seemed neutral. There was a subtle shift in her eye color—a glint of deeper gray if she was appeasing, and a lighter sparkle if she truly agreed.

Today, her eyes sparkled like early morning dew. I felt a wave of relief wash over me.

Molly was robust in her pride of etiquette and virtue, the epitome of reliability. In a household where I often found myself at odds with Sally and Louisa, Molly's steadfast loyalty was my refuge.

"He is, isn't he?" My voice bubbled like a cheerful brook, even as Molly tugged a horsehair brush through my long red locks. The silver backing of the brush caught the warm glow of the kerosene lamp, scattering light like tiny starbursts across the mirror. "I can't believe I didn't see it from the beginning. I was so determined to disagree with Father. You see, I wasn't wrong about my position—arranged marriages are archaic—but I was wrong about Daniel. He's a worthy gentleman. Kind, humorous, and unbelievably patient with Louisa."

Molly's mouth twitched with amusement at my girlish enthusiasm. With anyone else, I might have felt embarrassed, but in the privacy of my room, I was free to express my feelings.

"Being in love is so exhilarating!" I exclaimed. "I must repent for all the disparaging thoughts I've had—albeit quietly —about romantic novels and love songs. It's all real, isn't it?"

"Of course it is, miss." Molly smiled as she began twisting my hair into a bun, pinning it in place with precision.

The mention of romance made me think of my mother. The shift in my emotions was sudden and sharp. "I so wish Mother were here," I said, my voice trembling. "She'd be so happy for me."

"She surely would, miss," Molly said softly.

"How awful it will be to marry without her." A lump formed in my throat. "Who will help me with my dress? The decorations? The festivities?"

"Mrs. Hartigan is sure to be helpful," Molly offered.

I let out a huff. "Only because it will raise her social standing. She doesn't care about my happiness."

Molly paused, placing the brush gently on the vanity. She met my gaze in the mirror with quiet determination. "I'm here, miss. I know I'm not your mother, but I care about your happiness. I'll help you in any way I can."

Before I realized it, I'd sprung up from my chair and thrown my arms around her neck. "Oh, Molly."

Molly returned my embrace with maternal grace, patting my back gently. "Now, now, miss," she murmured.

When I pulled away, I found tears streaking my cheeks. "I don't know what's come over me."

"You're acting quite normally, miss," Molly said with a knowing smile. "You're about to become a wife and soon after, a mother. It's a big change. It's only natural to feel a bit overwhelmed."

She helped me into my corset, pulling the strings firmly as I held my breath. Next came the emerald silk skirt, embellished with lace embroidery, and the matching blouse, which buttoned all the way up to my chin. Molly tied a dark green sash snugly around my waist, completing the ensemble.

A wife. A mother. The thought filled me with both joy and longing. Oh, how I missed Daniel! It had been only two weeks since he left for England, yet each day felt heavier than the last. How would I make it through the long winter months without him?

"I think I'd like to wear Mother's locket," I said suddenly. Father had given me the gold locket years ago. I rarely wore it, often choosing more fashionable pieces, but today, I wanted something of hers close to me, even if it remained hidden beneath my blouse.

"A very good idea," Molly said, crossing the room to fetch it from my jewelry box. As she rummaged through its contents, her expression shifted from calm to perplexed. "It's not here, miss."

"Not there?" I asked, frowning. "That's where I last saw it."

"I thought so as well," Molly said, her chin lifting slightly. "Perhaps it's been misplaced."

We spent the next hour searching my room. Every drawer was opened and sifted through. Dresses were inspected, and pockets turned out. Handbags were emptied, and shoes upturned. Molly even crawled under the bed, muttering something about dust bunnies that would shame Mrs. Hartigan.

At last, we sat on the edge of the bed, defeated. "Molly," I said slowly, my voice tinged with dread, "I think someone's taken it."

Her eyes widened in shock. "Not me, miss!"

"Of course not," I said quickly.

But the unpleasant truth was undeniable: someone in the household had likely stolen it. My mind raced through the possibilities. Mrs. Bakker, the cook, was always trustworthy, but what about the scullery maid, June? Or Wendy, the parlor maid? Then there was Father's new chauffeur, Cuthbert, who had only been with us a few months. Any of them could have furtively wandered into my room and taken the locket, mistaking it for a piece no one would miss.

The realization hit me like a slap. I can't rule out anyone—not even Molly.

I glanced at her out of the corner of my eye, her kind face drawn in concern. My heart ached at the thought, but fairness demanded I consider every possibility. Still, the idea of Molly—who had been my rock for over a decade—stealing from me felt impossible.

"We'll find it, miss," Molly said firmly, breaking the silence. "And if someone has taken it, they'll have to answer for it."

Her words bolstered my confidence, though the seed of doubt had been planted. I resolved to conduct a quiet inquiry, beginning with the staff. But for now, I smoothed my skirt, lifted my chin, and said, "Let's not speak of this to anyone just yet."

Molly nodded. "As you wish, miss."

Despite her agreement, I couldn't shake the unease settling over me. The locket isn't just a piece of jewelry—it's a connection to my mother, to my past, and to the woman I hope to become. Though it pierces my heart to do so, I have to add Molly to the list of suspects.

Chapter Nine

THE CIGAR CASE

November 9, 1912

TODAY, I visited Father in his study, where a number of disturbing events unfolded. He looked sharp in his navy pinstriped suit, seated at his mahogany desk with his spectacles propped on his nose. A newspaper lay spread in his hands.

"I hope Woodrow is watching the Baltic closely," he muttered.

I delivered a cup of hot coffee, setting it on the desk, then perched myself in a leather wingback chair. "What do you mean?" I asked.

"The Balkan states mean to drive out the Ottoman Empire —an empire that has ruled for six hundred years. The unrest in Europe makes me uneasy."

"I'm sure it's unpleasant for the people who live there," I said, hoping to sound sympathetic.

Father lowered the paper, dipping his chin to peer at me

over his spectacles. "It's a tinderbox that could start a forest fire."

"Surely, it's not as bad as all that," I replied. "Hopefully, it will end quickly."

Father grunted. While I sympathized with the struggles of those in Eastern Europe, it seemed inconceivable that their troubles could affect us so far away in America.

Lifting his cup of coffee, Father's hand suddenly trembled so badly he had to set it down. Coffee sloshed into the saucer. Alarmed, I stared, but Father ignored me, letting the newspaper fall to the desk. Using both hands, he lifted the cup again and took a sip.

"Are you all right?" I asked, my voice tight with concern.

"Of course," he replied, waving off my worry. "I slept on my arm the wrong way last night. Pinched a nerve, I suspect."

"Shall I call for the doctor?"

"No need," he said sharply. He set the cup down with steadier hands. "Now, where is my cigar case?"

Father's silver cigar case was a gift from my mother early in their marriage. It's shaped like three tubes joined together to hold three cigars, and a riot of engraved flowers and vines chase each other over the outside. In the center of the lid are a prominent G and H, my father's initials. It is a conversation starter and one of his most prized belongings. He patted his vest, checked his desk drawers, and frowned.

"When did you last see it?" I asked, joining the search.

"I can't rightly remember."

"Think back. Was it yesterday? Last week?"

"I'm not sure. Wednesday, perhaps. I've been smoking less lately."

I blinked in surprise. Father, who found such joy in his regular cigars, once again looked older, his jowls sagging. The lines on his face were deeper, his skin ruddy, and his hair thinner. When had that happened?

Pushing the thought aside, I focused on the task at hand. "Who's been in your study since then?"

Father frowned. "No visitors. Just the household staff."

My stomach lurched as I remembered my missing locket, which Molly and I had searched for to no avail.

"Besides Sally and Louisa, has anyone else been here?"

"The door is often unlocked," Father admitted. "The maids come in to clean and start the fire. Mrs. Bakker sometimes brings me a slice of cake—she likes to see my reaction, which is always positive."

"Mrs. Bakker is an exceptional baker," I agreed, though my thoughts lingered elsewhere. "What about Cuthbert?"

Father's new chauffeur is a new hire. Nothing went missing before he came.

"Cuthbert came with the highest recommendation."

Hadn't all our employees? I kept the observation to myself.

Father sighed, giving up the search. "Never mind it for now, I'll use the cigars from the larger box. Oh, but I'm out of matches."

"I'll fetch some for you," I offered.

"Thank you, Ginger. I'd best get back to work."

I found Cuthbert in the servants' quarters, laughing with the maids. When they noticed me, June and Wendy scurried off like frightened mice while Cuthbert froze, staring over my head. I was grateful I'd chosen my blue silk dress with its modern square-cut neckline and contrasting yellow sash—it made me feel confident enough to confront him.

"Mr. Cuthbert," I began. "My father can't find his cigar case. Have you seen it?"

"I'm not certain I know the case you mean, madam," he said evenly.

I narrowed my eyes, unconvinced. "It's silver, with a distinctive design and his initials on the lid."

Recognition flickered in his expression. "Ah, yes. I've seen it—a lovely piece."

"It's missing."

Cuthbert straightened. "Shall I search the carriage? It might have fallen out of Mr. Hartigan's pocket."

"Please do," I said curtly.

Cuthbert left, and I lingered in the servants' dining room, listening to the sounds of the household. From the kitchen, Sally's sharp voice filtered through as she gave Mrs. Bakker instructions for the evening meal. My stomach sank when she entered the room just as Cuthbert returned, slightly out of breath.

"I'm afraid it's not in the carriage, madam," he reported.

"What's going on here?" Sally's voice had that edge that always put me on guard.

"Ginger? What are you and Cuthbert up to?"

Her use of my familiar name in front of Father's chauffeur grated on me. I was engaged to be married, for crying out loud!

"We're not 'up to' anything, Mrs. Hartigan," I said coolly, deliberately emphasizing her formal title. She didn't seem to notice.

"Father's cigar case is missing," I explained, "and I'm trying to recover it."

Sally scoffed. "It hasn't gone missing. He's simply misplaced it." Sally has always been jealous of how fond Father is of that cigar case, as it's a keepsake of my mother. She turned her glare on Cuthbert. "Surely you have something useful to do."

"Y-yes, ma'am," he stammered.

I watched him retreat, wondering what else he could possibly do besides waiting for Father to require his services.

Mrs. Bakker produced a box of matches upon request, and I delivered it to Father as promised.

I'm no closer to solving the mystery, but one thing is certain: Mr. Cuthbert had better be on his best behavior. I'll be keeping a very close eye on him from now on.

Chapter Ten

TO CATCH A THIEF

December 1, 1912

I WAS DRAWN downstairs to the kitchen this morning by the unmistakable and irresistible aroma of sugar cookies. The sweet, buttery scent stirred up comforting memories of my childhood—those early days of homesickness after leaving London when Mrs. Beasley, our cook, would take me under her wing. Mrs. Bakker even let me help decorate the cookies, though I was sworn to keep it a secret from Sally.

As I grew older, I made fewer trips to the kitchen, adopting the more proper habits of a young lady. But the smell of sugar cookies was enough to overcome my adult sensibilities, and my legs carried me downstairs before I could think twice.

When I reached the foot of the stairs, I heard voices. One was unmistakably Cuthbert's and the other was the parlor maid, Wendy, giggling softly.

"Miss Powell," Cuthbert said, his voice smooth, "there's a

barn dance in Cambridge this weekend, and it would please me greatly if you'd agree to be my escort."

Wendy giggled again. "All right," she replied coyly, "but only if you walk me back home by ten. It wouldn't be proper otherwise."

Cuthbert clicked his tongue. "All prim and proper, eh? Well, if you insist."

More giggles followed, and I smiled. Romance, it seemed, was not confined to social class. I missed Daniel terribly and would give anything to have him here. I'd even agree to attend a barn dance if it meant being by his side.

"I do have a small favor to ask, Miss Powell, if you don't mind?"

I felt a twinge of guilt for eavesdropping. If I continued into the kitchen, they'd surely see me, but retreating meant making noise on the creaky steps. Torn, I decided to stay where I was, listening quietly.

"Oh, I couldn't," Wendy said suddenly, her giggles replaced by a nervous tremor.

"It's just a small thing," Cuthbert pressed. His tone turned coaxing, almost syrupy. "They wouldn't even miss it. It's not like the family is short on money. Think of it as a little bonus to our wages."

I froze, my chest tightening with fury. Cuthbert was the thief! And now he was trying to drag poor Wendy into his schemes.

"Mr. Cuthbert!" Wendy exclaimed, her voice filled with distress. I imagined her cupping her hands over her mouth in horror.

Cuthbert chuckled darkly. "I was only joking, Miss Powell. You should see your face. What a relief you said no—I'd hate to have to report you to Mr. Hartigan."

The nerve! First, he tries to corrupt Wendy, and then he

insinuates she's the one in the wrong. My forgotten craving for sugar cookies was replaced by a fiery determination to catch Cuthbert in the act.

I spent the rest of the day quietly observing him, altering my routine to stay near his whereabouts. When he went to polish the carriage, I wandered into the garden, ostensibly to snip flowers. When he returned to the servants' quarters to polish boots, I found an excuse to visit the kitchen and request a special dish from Mrs. Beasley.

It struck me that Cuthbert would likely wait until dinner to make his move. With the family gathered in the dining room, Sally's bedroom would be unguarded. Wendy's duty to clean it each morning made her a convenient target for Cuthbert's charm.

Determined, I recruited Molly to help.

"Are you sure you heard him right, miss?" she asked, her brow furrowing.

"There's no mistaking his intentions," I replied. "The linen closet is just down the hall from Sally's room. I need you to wait there with the door ajar and watch for Cuthbert."

"You want me to hide in the closet?" Molly asked, incredulous.

"Yes. It's unconventional, but Father and Sally would notice my absence at dinner. If you see him enter Sally's room, come down to the dining room and give me a sign. I'll come up straight away."

Molly hesitated, biting her lip. "Are you sure this will work, miss? It could be dangerous."

"Catching him snooping in Sally's room is all we need. With you as my witness, he won't be able to deny it. Tonight will be the last we see of Mr. Cuthbert."

My plan worked perfectly. As I suspected, Cuthbert made his move during dinner. Molly waved at me from the door of the dining room, and I slipped away, convincing Sally to join me for good measure.

The look on Cuthbert's face when we caught him in Sally's room was priceless. Standing there with my stepmother's pearls draped over his arm, he froze like a deer in the hunter's sights.

"Put down my pearls at once!" Sally demanded, her voice sharp with fury.

Cuthbert dropped the pearls and shoved past us, nearly knocking Sally over. "Stop him!" she cried.

We rushed after him, our commotion drawing Father and Louisa to the bottom of the staircase.

"What's going on?" Father asked just as Cuthbert missed a step and tumbled down the stairs. I gasped, first at the fall and then at the sight of his trousers—split clean down the back seam.

Louisa howled with laughter. "He ripped his pants!"

Cuthbert scrambled to his feet, clutching at his torn trousers as he bolted through the green baize door.

"What on earth just happened?" Father demanded, his gaze bouncing between us.

"Cuthbert is a thief," I declared. "We must notify the police. Perhaps we can retrieve your cigar case and my locket."

The constable arrived shortly after to take our statements, and to our delight, when he searched Cuthbert's room, he found my locket and Father's cigar case hidden in the back of Cuthbert's dresser drawer. It marked an end to what was undoubtedly one of the most exciting evenings the Hartigan household had seen in months. I have to admit, the chase gave me a bit of a thrill.

Later that night, as I sat in my room reflecting on the day's events, Molly knocked gently on my door.

"Miss Hartigan, the mail came this evening, and with all the excitement, I forgot to give you this." She handed me an envelope bearing the distinct postal markings of the Royal Mail Service and a stamp with the image of the King.

My heart raced. "Thank you, Molly."

I waited until she left before tearing open the letter. My hands trembled as I unfolded the pages, my eyes drinking in the familiar penmanship.

My Dearest Georgia,

I am a hollow shell without you by my side. Since I met you, I have not been the same. I am incomplete. I count the days until we are together again, and I can make you my wife.

Until then, we must rely on letters—a desperately slow and inadequate way to connect, yet alas, my love, it is our only way for now.

Enough of my pining and complaints. To take our minds off the ocean that separates us, let me tell you about life at Bray Manor.

It is cold here, with winter pressing in, though not as cold as I hear it is there. I do hope we get some snow this year, at least in time for Christmas. Meanwhile, we have our normal, wet, grey winter weather.

Felicia, it must be said, is enjoying the rain, stomping through puddles with great delight, whenever she is taken outside for her walk. I bought her a pink brolly—umbrella, in case you've forgotten how to "speak Brit"—with butterflies on it, so there is no holding her back. Grandmother disapproves, but with a good pair of galoshes to keep Felicia's feet dry, I don't see why at least one of us shouldn't be able to get some enjoyment out of this season.

Speaking of Grandmother, she is too proud to express her gratitude for your father's generosity in virtually saving Bray

Manor, but I can see the weight that has been lifted from her shoulders, and for that, I am grateful.

Don't get me wrong, the Dowager Lady Ambrosia Gold is no delicate flower. She has a mind full of opinions, which she freely shares. Just yesterday, she declared, "Bray Manor will never be outfitted with electricity! God made the sun, and if it's good enough for Him, it's good enough for us!"

I couldn't help but laugh, especially as the proper cleaning of the lamps in the Manor is one of the points Grandmother is a terror on—but apparently lamps do not count as being contrary to God's creation of sunlight. She is quite a character, and I cannot wait for you to meet her.

Bray Manor itself is damp and cold. Much as I enjoy a good blaze in the fireplace, it does tend to roast you in the front and freeze you in the back; the central heating you have in some houses in America is much more convenient. But I won't complain. We are warm, fed, and in good health. Despite its faults, I am deeply fond of my childhood home and look forward to sharing it with you on our wedding journey. Thankfully, it will be summertime by then!

Have a happy Christmas, my love. This will be the last one we spend apart. I look forward to many happy Christmases together in the years to come, growing old and grey side by side. And how exciting it will be when the children come—what joy they will bring!

With all my love and devotion,
  Daniel

P.S. Please write soon.

Chapter Eleven

THE WINTER COAT

December 24, 1912

It's a Hartigan family tradition to volunteer at Christ Church on Salem Street every Christmas Eve to help serve dinner to Boston's poor and underprivileged citizens—a charitable effort driven by my warm-hearted father and resisted with equal determination by my headstrong stepmother, Sally.

"The church is doing just fine without me having to get my gloves dirty," Sally said as we sat around the warmth of the fire in the sitting room. "Can't we enjoy a quiet, carefree Christmas Eve for once, George?"

"We are blessed beyond measure," Father replied, as he did every year. "Christmas is about giving, and as members of the elite, it's doubly important we remember those whose lives are a daily struggle."

Sally wasn't ready to concede. "Think about Louisa."

At the mention of her name, Louisa glanced up from the porcelain doll she'd been playing with.

"Would you have your young daughter exposed to who-knows-what ailment? Last year, a man stood right behind her and coughed."

I noticed Sally's careful phrasing: your young daughter. She didn't seem concerned that someone might inadvertently cough in my direction.

"I do think about Louisa, which is exactly why I insist on going," Father said firmly.

"I'm not sure we're doing those people much good," Sally continued. "They'll just learn to depend on handouts."

"It's Christmas," I interjected, siding with Father.

Sally's nose jutted higher. "They're immigrants."

I was aghast. "We're immigrants!"

Louisa smirked. "I'm not."

Father wasn't swayed, and at five o'clock that evening, the four of us bundled into our fur-trimmed winter coats, muffs, and hats, and rode in our enclosed carriage as the new driver directed the horses to the church hall.

Boston is breathtaking in the winter twilight, with snow falling softly and glowing like fairy lights beneath the gas lamps. The air was crisp and cold, our breaths curling in visible wisps. Sally sat rigidly, her face pinched with disapproval, while Louisa made chugging sounds, mimicking a steam engine with the puffs of her breath.

"Louisa!" Sally snapped. "Stop that childish nonsense."

"She is a child," I said, defending my sister. "And it's Christmastime. Let her enjoy her imagination."

Sally snarled. "Who are you to tell me how to manage my daughter?"

"Her sister," I replied uncharitably. It wasn't my finest moment.

"Sally, girls," Father admonished. "Please, let's try to get along. This is the season of peace and goodwill."

The rest of the ride passed in silence. I focused again on the magical world beyond the carriage. The streets were quieter than usual, the snow muffling sound with an ethereal peace. Passersby offered smiles, waves, and cheerful cries of "Merry Christmas!" I soon forgot my spat with Sally and returned the greetings. "Merry Christmas!"

Oh, how I missed Daniel. I kept reminding myself that by next Christmas, I would be a married woman—perhaps even with a little one on the way. The thought warmed me against the Boston chill and filled me with anticipation for the year to come.

Not everyone shared in the season's cheer. As our carriage moved further north, the streets grew rougher, and the number of vagrants increased. Many wore layers of mismatched, tattered clothing, rubbing their hands together for warmth as they huddled around garbage cans from which flames flickered.

One woman caught my eye. She stood near a fire, her dark, lifeless gaze meeting mine through the carriage window. Her coat, narrow at the waist and hopelessly outdated, was threadbare and ill-suited to ward off the biting cold. In contrast, I sat swathed in my Parisian wool coat with its wide fur-trimmed collar, cuffs, and hem. Guilt pressed heavily on me.

"But by the grace of God," Father said quietly, "there go I."

"I really don't like it when you say that," Sally said sharply. "Where is the grace of God for them?"

"God's grace is for all and can be found by anyone," Father replied. "I suspect the least among us have a keener knowledge of that grace."

"I don't understand why we have to go to them, Father," Louisa piped up. "We have plenty of money. Can't we just give some of that to the church? I'm cold, and I want to go home."

"There's sense talking," Sally said approvingly.

"We could give money," Father acknowledged, "but where

would be the reward? It is, after all, better to give than to receive."

"As Louisa astutely pointed out," Sally said, "we can give money."

Father smiled gently. "But the giving of one's time and the offering of one's compassion are where true rewards are found."

He cast a smile my way. I knew that he also gave money to the poor, and not just at Christmastime.

At the church hall, Reverend Wilson greeted us warmly, shaking hands with each of us.

"God bless you for volunteering at such a meaningful time as this," he said sincerely. "Christmas can be especially hard for those already struggling. Please, come in!"

Father and I helped in the kitchen, while Sally and Louisa "helped" serve coffee and cake. I use the word "helped" charitably, because they mostly hovered, grimacing at the guests with thinly veiled disapproval.

Among the guests, I recognized the woman from the street. Up close, she looked frail—her bony fingers trembling as she held a cup of coffee, her dark eyes shadowed with exhaustion. Despite the warmth of the hall, she hadn't removed her coat. I realized with alarm that it was so threadbare that it couldn't possibly protect her against the Boston cold.

I hurried to the back room, where the staff kept their belongings, retrieved my coat, and returned to the hall. For a moment, I panicked when I couldn't find her, but then a larger man moved aside, and there she was.

I approached her hesitantly. "Hello. I'm Miss Hartigan."

"Ma'am," she said. "Name's Parker."

"Pleased to meet you, Mrs. Parker. I hope I'm not being too forward, but I wondered if you'd like this." I held up my coat.

Her bewildered eyes darted between me and the garment. "Whatcha mean?"

"It's a Christmas present. For you."

Her gaze lingered on the coat with longing. I couldn't imagine the last time she'd felt truly warm.

"Please, try it on," I coaxed. She extended a thin arm, but before she could put it on, Sally's sharp voice rang out.

"Ginger Hartigan! What on earth are you doing?"

I turned, steeling myself. "I'm giving this lady my coat."

"Stop it this instant! It's brand new—from Filene's!"

"I'll just get another one," I said firmly.

Sally's obstinacy knew no bounds. "She'll just sell it."

"It's hers to do with as she pleases," I replied, just as stubbornly.

Mrs. Parker tried to hand the coat back. "I can't accept it, miss."

"Yes, you can," I insisted. I soften my gaze and gripped her bare hand, thin and cold. "Please. It's yours."

Her dark eyes shone with gratitude. "Thank you, miss. I promise to help someone else, just like you helped me."

She slipped into the coat, fiddling with the buttons. For the first time, a smile lit her face.

Sally stormed off to Father, no doubt expecting him to chastise me. Instead, he smiled warmly when he heard what I'd done.

"Oh, Ginger, my love. I'm so proud of you."

My heart swelled with love for my father. I threw my arms around him, grateful beyond words.

Chapter Twelve

CRACKER JACKS

February 11, 1913

I AM a silly goose when it comes to Daniel. As I pressed his most recent letter to my chest, I couldn't keep my joy inside. My heart felt like it might burst from my happiness.

"He'll be here in three weeks, Molly. Three weeks!"

Molly's lips twitched with a restrained smile, but her eyes sparkled with genuine pleasure at my good news. "I'm sure we'll all be relieved when he arrives safely, Miss Hartigan."

"I think I'm going to explode with happiness," I said, twirling in front of my vanity. "I simply can't contain it. You know what this means, Molly?"

Molly raised an eyebrow, her hands stilling as she folded a fresh stack of linens. "I should get my coat?"

"Yes! We must go shopping! I can't have Daniel see me in this old thing." I gestured dramatically to my long-sleeved blue silk dress, with its narrow waist and elaborate lace trim, that I had bought some six weeks ago.

Molly's lips pressed together in an effort not to roll her eyes. "Old, you say?"

Well, be that as it may, shopping was a necessity—or so I convinced myself. A girl must shop when a girl must shop!

Even though Molly is my maid, I prefer her company when shopping over inviting a friend. Shopping with friends always comes with an unspoken competition: who can find the most exquisite dress or hat first, and, more importantly, who looks the best in it? That kind of strain doesn't exist with Molly. She never shops in the stores where I shop, anyway.

Re-reading the previous paragraph of my entry, I realize how conceited that sounds. But truly, Molly is wonderful company. I think she enjoys the outings, too—after all, she gets to escape the household routine for a few hours. And she has good taste; I think she enjoys seeing the beautiful materials and styles on display.

When I announced my plans to Father, he shook his head with an amused grin. "One might freeze to death, but that's all nought in pursuit of the perfect frock," he said, his English accent like warm honey to my ears.

"Oh, Father! It's cold, but not so cold as to keep us indoors."

Father instructed our new driver, McDoogle, to bring the carriage around and put some hot bricks in to warm our feet.

"Where to, miss?" McDoogle asked with a thick Irish brogue as he helped Molly and me climb into the carriage. He was a rotund man with ruddy cheeks framed by dark mutton-chop whiskers, his bowler hat perched atop a shock of unruly hair. He wore a scarf and wool coat, tall boots, and gloves that looked as though they'd seen better days.

"Filene's on Washington Street, please," I said cheerfully.

We arrived at the grand department store in no time. After arranging for McDoogle to pick us up in two hours, I took

Molly's arm, and we hurried inside, our breaths forming frosty puffs in the cold winter air.

"You must be my objective observer," I said once we were safely indoors. The warmth of the store wrapped around us like a woolen blanket. "The store clerks only tell me what they think I want to hear to make a sale."

Molly smiled faintly. "I'll do my best, miss, but you know I'm not well-versed in what's fashionable."

"You have good instincts," I insisted. "Besides, you know me and what I like."

"Thank you, miss," Molly replied.

Finding the perfect item proved more difficult than I'd anticipated. I tried on a parade of dresses and hats, each one more elaborate than the last. After an hour, I was thoroughly exhausted but finally settled on a green wool dress and a spectacular wide-brimmed hat trimmed with a broad white silk ribbon.

Molly's faint nod of approval confirmed my choice.

Outside the store, we passed a young boy selling candy from a small stall tucked into an alcove. He was bundled in a patched up coat and woolen cap, his cheeks pink from the cold.

"Look, Molly!" I said, pointing to the boxes of Cracker Jack candy. "Baseball fans adore these. Have you ever had a box?"

Molly shook her head. "No, Miss Hartigan, I haven't had the pleasure."

"It's popcorn and peanuts coated in caramel," I explained, purchasing two boxes. I opened one and dug through the popcorn until I found the small toy hidden inside. "A cat charm! How sweet. Louisa will love it. Oh, I'd better buy another box for her, or she'll never forgive me."

As we nibbled on the sticky-sweet treat, Molly remarked, "This is very good, miss. I see why it's so popular."

"It's part of the song they play at baseball games," I said, breaking into a grin.

Like schoolgirls, we began to sing:

> *"Take me out to the ball game,*
> *Take me out with the crowd;*
> *Buy me some peanuts and Cracker Jack,*
> *I don't care if I never get back.*
> *Let me root, root, root for the home team,*
> *If they don't win, it's a shame.*
> *For it's one, two, three strikes, you're out,*
> *At the old ball game!"*

We finished with a fit of laughter.

"Oh, Molly," I said, catching my breath. "That reminds me of Daniel and the time we went to Fenway Park. What a day that was!"

Molly's smile softened. "It's going to be a very long three weeks for you, isn't it, Miss Hartigan?"

"You're absolutely right, Molly," I said with a wistful sigh.

McDoogle arrived promptly at the arranged time, and I handed him my new hatbox and the big box that contained my new dress, before climbing into the carriage with Molly's help.

Back at home, Louisa's reaction to the Cracker Jack box was everything I'd anticipated. She gasped with delight when I handed it to her.

"Oh, thank you, Ginger!" she cried, tearing it open. She sifted through the popcorn and found the toy charm inside. "A dog! Look, it's a little dog!"

I smiled. Her joy was infectious. Father, observing from his armchair, chuckled. "You've made her day, Ginger."

"It's the least I could do," I said, taking a seat by the fire. I removed the wide-brimmed hat from its box, placing it carefully on my head. "Do you approve, Father?"

He tilted his head thoughtfully. "You'll look lovely when Daniel arrives."

My heart swelled with excitement. Three weeks felt like an eternity, but the thought of Daniel's arrival made the wait worthwhile.

Chapter Thirteen

DANIEL RETURNS

March 1, 1913

Daniel arrived today.

In my dreams and imagination, our reunion was nothing short of divine. He would step off the ship dressed in a crisp suit, a bowler hat perched perfectly on his blond head, and the sun glistening behind him like a halo. I, of course, would be the picture of elegance in the latest fashion: my sleek, tailored royal-blue wool suit—fresh from the Sears catalog—and a new military-style corset. My hem would fall neatly above my black, pointy-toed boots, and a black straw hat adorned with an oversized satin bow would complete the ensemble.

So dressed, I would glide toward him. Our eyes would meet, and the world around us would blur and disappear. We'd hurry into each other's arms, his hands cupping my face, and I'd shed tears of joy as we kissed.

That was my dream.

But real life, as always, had other plans.

I had intended to bring only Molly with me to meet Daniel at the docks, but Father insisted on coming as well. After all, Daniel wasn't just my fiancé—he was also Father's new business partner. Louisa overheard the conversation and threw one of her infamous tantrums.

"I like Daniel! I want to come too!" she shouted, cheeks flushed red as she jumped up and down, her boots thudding against the floorboards.

No amount of reasoning would calm her, and when Father finally relented, it meant Sally had to join us as well.

I protested vehemently. "There'll be no room for Daniel in the carriage!"

Father smiled with maddening patience. "I'll give McDoogle the day off and drive the carriage myself. Daniel can sit up front with me. It's a lovely day, and we'll have plenty to talk about."

"But he's come for me!" I couldn't hide my frustration. "Daniel should ride in the carriage with me!"

Father chuckled, which only infuriated me more. "There'll be plenty of time for the two of you to be together, love. For now, let's be practical."

And so, there we were: Father, Sally, Louisa, Molly, and I crammed into the carriage, heading for Boston Harbor.

The sight of the ocean liner growing larger on the horizon was nothing short of majestic. Its three enormous black-and-red smokestacks sent billows of steam spiraling into the sky, resembling giant candles snuffed out by an invisible hand. The air was crisp and cold, tinged with the briny smell of the sea mingling unpleasantly with the stench of fish from Quincy Market.

As passengers began to disembark in a thick crowd, a blur of hats and parasols, Louisa pointed excitedly.

"Is that him?"

I turned quickly in the direction she indicated, my heart racing—only to feel a pang of disappointment when I saw no one familiar.

"Oh, I thought I saw him," Louisa said with a pout, and I bit my tongue to keep from snapping at her. She had raised my hopes for nothing.

We waited and waited, and with each passing moment, my doubts grew. My boots, tied too tightly in my haste that morning, pinched my feet painfully. The early spring chill turned the tip of my nose red—so red that I dared to cross my eyes briefly to confirm it.

Where was Daniel?

Perhaps he'd missed the boat in Liverpool and hadn't managed to send a telegram. Or worse, perhaps he had changed his mind. I tried to shake the thought, but it lingered like a shadow over my joy. Was the price of marriage to me too high to save Bray Manor? Had he found another way to secure his family's fortunes?

As if reading my thoughts, Molly patted my shoulder. "He'll be here shortly," she said, her soft brogue slipping into her voice—a sure sign she was worried.

Sally seized the opportunity to make things worse. "Look at her, George," she said to Father. "I told you she wasn't ready for this."

"I'm ready!" I snapped, glaring at her. In truth, I was ready to leave her house and establish my own. That was what I was ready for!

My throat was dry, my eyes watered from frustration, and I felt on the verge of tears when—finally—I spotted him.

There was no halo.

Daniel looked tired and worn, his usual confident posture sagging slightly. He was pale, his expression weary, and I recalled reading about the storm that had battered the Atlantic. He wasn't in tip-top shape, but he was here.

He shook Father's hand, tipped his hat politely to Sally and Louisa, and greeted Molly with his usual charm.

And then his eyes met mine. He smiled—a soft, genuine smile—but the world didn't fall away as I had imagined. There was no grand embrace, no cupped hands on my face. Instead, Louisa's giggles echoed loudly, completely ruining the moment.

Worst of all, I froze. After five long months of longing for Daniel's return, he stood before me, and I couldn't move or speak. Shyness overwhelmed me, and I felt like a statue.

Molly, ever the hero, saved the day. "Well, the wind is brisk," she said. "Cook has a warm meal waiting."

Daniel and Father walked ahead of us as the porter struggled with Daniel's luggage. I climbed into the carriage alongside Molly, sitting opposite Sally and Louisa. Oddly, I felt relieved that Daniel was riding up front with Father.

"You'll warm up over time," Molly whispered kindly, her gaze steady. "He loves you."

I nodded. I knew it was true. His letters had left no doubt in my mind. We just needed time to reacquaint ourselves.

But Sally, of course, couldn't let me have a moment of peace. "You think he's marrying you for love?" she whispered harshly. "Believe me, marriage is a business contract. You're nothing more than a railcar of steel or a stock number to him."

Her words hit like a slap. But this time, I found my voice.

"Maybe that was true for you, Sally," I said, keeping my voice low while glaring at her. "But I'll marry for love—or not at all!"

Her sharp intake of breath told me I'd struck a nerve. Good. I swear, that woman brings out the worst in me.

Chapter Fourteen

VAUDEVILLE

March 8, 1912

LAST NIGHT, Daniel took me to a vaudeville theater! I'd heard of the vaudeville craze, of course, and knew there were several theaters near the Boston Common, but I'd never dared to visit one, so when Daniel suggested an evening at B.F. Keith's Theater, my eyebrows nearly shot off my forehead.

"Vaudeville?" I asked, unable to hide my skepticism.

Like most proper young ladies, I had been warned about the reputation of such venues. The bawdy dance shows, risqué humor, and questionable clientele had firmly secured vaudeville's place on the list of things I was meant to avoid. This suggestion made me wonder if I'd ever known Daniel at all.

Daniel's face registered my hesitation, and he was quick to respond. "You're worried about it being too much, I can tell. It was so in the early days, but the routines have changed over the years." His tone was reassuring. "I've met the owner of this particular theater—

B.F. Keith himself—and he assured me his shows are suitable for ladies. Even children are welcome at certain matinees."

He hesitated before adding, "Your father has given his blessing, provided you agree to accompany me."

My mind raced—not about the vaudeville show itself but about the prospect of being alone with Daniel. Since his return, I have gone to great lengths to ensure we were always in the company of others. Louisa, in particular, had been all too eager to act as a chaperone.

Daniel must have noticed my hesitation. Anxiety flashed behind his eyes before he quickly replaced it with a smile. "If there's even a hint of salaciousness, I promise we'll leave at once."

What does one wear to an event where one might have to flee in haste?

"All right," I said at last, determined to put him at ease. After all, he was my fiancé. How could I refuse?

The evening began with our arrival at B.F. Keith's Theater, which is situated across from the Boston Common on Tremont Street. The air was brisk, and the sun was just beginning to set, casting a golden glow over the impressive brick and stone building.

As we stepped from the carriage, I couldn't help but admire the enormous marquee announcing the evening's performers in bold lettering: "Eddie Foy and the Seven Little Foys!"

Daniel gestured toward the sign. "It's a song-and-dance act performed by a man and his seven children," he explained. "They're known for their clever humor and impressive choreography."

Other acts listed on the marquee included the comedic duo Clarke and Bergman, the Yiddish singer Belle Baker, and, according to Daniel, the possibility of circus acts like jugglers or contortionists.

The theater itself was nothing short of magnificent. The foyer was grand, with high ceilings adorned by crystal chandeliers. Plush carpeting muffled our footsteps as we admired the beautifully painted walls, one of which featured an extraordinary piece by the Italian artist V. Tojetti.

We ascended the grand staircase to the main seating area, where a sign at the top made me smile: "No smoking, whistling, foot-stamping, spitting, or crunching of peanuts anywhere in the building. Foul language is strictly prohibited."

Daniel had reserved a private box to the right of the stage. The seats were velvet with high backs and armrests, and I couldn't help but feel like royalty as I gazed down at the audience below. It was then that the weight of my circumstances struck me.

Daniel wasn't just any man. He was a baron, and when I married him, I would become a "Lady." Though Americans didn't put much stock in titles, I knew that being a baroness was a position of great importance.

When I married Daniel.

Why did those words fill me with such fear?

Daniel must have sensed my unease because he leaned toward me and spoke softly. "Georgia, love, have you changed your mind?"

"What do you mean?"

"About us. About getting married. To me."

My heart pounded, and my throat went dry. Had I? Had I changed my mind?

Daniel reached for my hand. "It's all right if you have," he said gently. "I understand. We barely know each other, and I've been away for so long. Perhaps you've met someone else?"

"No!" The word came out with such force that I startled

myself. "I want to marry you," I added quickly, realizing at that moment how true it was. Daniel's willingness to let me walk away—even knowing the cost to his family—only cemented my love for him. He is a good man, the kind of man I want to spend my life with.

"I'm sorry I haven't been able to express it," I continued, feeling I owed him an explanation. "I've been shy, and I suppose I've let that get in the way."

Daniel smiled, his hand tightening gently around mine. "It's one thing to get to know a fellow and another thing entirely to agree to marry him." He hesitated before adding, "If you'd feel better, we could postpone the wedding."

For a brief moment, I considered the idea. But the thought of delaying our August nuptials was unbearable.

"I want to marry you this summer," I said, leaning in to kiss him softly on the cheek. "I do."

Daniel's face lit up with a smile that made my heart swell. "Splendid! You've made me the happiest man alive."

Before we could say more—or risk embarrassing ourselves with a public display of affection—the lights dimmed, and the curtain rose.

The evening's performances were a delight. Eddie Foy and the Seven Little Foys were charming, with six-year-old Irving stealing the show with his antics. Their singing and dancing were impeccable, and I couldn't help but imagine the children Daniel and I might have someday—a lively little clan of Golds.

Of course, thinking too hard about how children come into existence made me blush furiously, even in the darkness of the theater. I could almost hear my father's voice in my head: "Don't put the cart before the horse, Ginger."

I resolved then and there to focus on the present. Our courtship was still young, and there was plenty of time to think about the future. For now, I would savor the joy of getting to know the man I loved.

As the curtain fell and the audience erupted in applause, Daniel leaned close to me once more. "So, my lady," he said with a teasing smile, "did the vaudeville theater pass your test?"

I laughed, feeling light and unburdened. "It was wonderful. Thank you for bringing me."

Daniel's eyes sparkled in the dim light. "I can't wait for all the adventures we'll share. This is just the beginning."

And for the first time, I truly believed it.

Chapter Fifteen

THE GRAND HECKLER

May 13, 1913

THIS WEEK, I witnessed an event destined to go down in history. Republican Senator Levi Greenwood gave a speech at Faneuil Hall in support of his re-election campaign for President of the Massachusetts State Senate. But it wasn't the speech itself that made the evening unforgettable—it was the chaos that followed.

Father and Daniel had planned to attend and didn't even bother to invite me! They simply assumed that, as a young lady, I wouldn't be interested in politics. Their oversight might have stung, but in this case, it worked to my advantage. Shortly after their departure, I received a note from my spirited friend Helen Ainsworth, brimming with intrigue.

Helen's message was clear: if I cared at all about the rights of women, I simply must join her at the rally. The Boston Equal Suffrage Association for Good Government (they call it

BESAGG) planned to make an appearance, and Margaret Foley —"The Grand Heckler" herself—would be there.

I confess, I didn't know who Margaret Foley was, though I wasn't about to reveal my ignorance to Helen.

When we met for tea at a cozy shop in Quincy Market an hour before the rally, Helen wasted no time enlightening me.

"Margaret Foley is a legend," Helen said, her eyes gleaming with admiration. "There are some in the suffrage association who think her tactics are too radical, but I find her utterly inspiring."

"What makes her so special?" I asked, eager to learn more.

Helen leaned forward as though sharing a great secret. "She's fearless. Politicians all over New England have felt the sting of her wit. She knows how to captivate a crowd, no matter how hostile."

I tried to imagine how one woman, armed only with words and a strong voice, could sway a roomful of men set in their ways. "Does she actually accomplish anything?"

Helen nodded emphatically. "Her Irish Catholic background makes her relatable to the working class, especially here in Boston. She's a force to be reckoned with."

The assembly hall at Faneuil Hall was packed to capacity by the time Senator Greenwood began his speech. The two-story brick building housed a bustling market on its ground floor, while the upper level served as a venue for political gatherings. Tonight, it brimmed with energy, the air thick with anticipation—and tension.

As Helen and I squeezed through the crowd to claim two hard wooden seats, I couldn't help noticing the glares from some of the men around us. It was clear we weren't welcome.

Senator Greenwood, a surprisingly youthful-looking man, began his speech with an air of confidence. "Fine citizens of Boston and my fellow Americans," he declared. "I am delighted to see such a robust turnout tonight. Your support over these last few years has been invaluable."

He paused for effect, then added, in a conspiratorial tone, "Men are fully capable of running the government and taking care of their women. Do women really need the vote to be protected by their men?"

Helen and I exchanged wide-eyed glances. He certainly wasn't wasting any time getting to the heart of the matter.

"Men have gone to war, endured every privation—even death itself—in defense of women," Greenwood continued. "While change is necessary, not all change is good. It takes forthright vision and courage to distinguish between progress and foolishness."

Suddenly, a tall woman rose from her seat about ten rows from the front. Her stylish stole and wide-brimmed hat set her apart, but it was her commanding voice that captured everyone's attention.

"Yes, Mr. Greenwood," she called out, her tone sharp and clear. "Change is on the horizon, and even a blind man can see it coming. How long will you cling to your fear of the women's vote? Do you think us stupid? Insipid? Your opponent, Mr. Edward Sibley, certainly does not!"

A ripple of shock passed through the audience as all eyes turned to her. Boldly, she stepped into the aisle, her voice growing stronger with each word.

"This man," she declared, gesturing toward Greenwood, "is known for his smooth rhetoric. But listen closely, and you'll hear the sound of a door closing. That door is closing on you, Mr. Greenwood."

Her words reverberated through the hall, her presence undeniable.

I flushed with a mix of admiration and second hand embarrassment. My eyes darted through the crowd, searching for my father and Daniel. What must they think of this audacious display? And more importantly, what did Daniel think about women's suffrage?

Greenwood responded with surprising composure. "Ah, Miss Foley," he said, his tone dripping with condescension. "How lovely of you to join us. It's always amusing to see a woman place her foot in her mouth while so nicely dressed!"

The crowd roared with laughter, emboldened by his mockery.

Foley didn't miss a beat. "Perhaps a foot in the mouth is better than two fingers in your ears, Mr. Greenwood," she shot back, earning a burst of laughter from the crowd—this time directed at the senator.

Undeterred, she continued, her voice unwavering. "Women deserve the vote so they can have a say in the taxes and laws that govern their lives. Perhaps then, even the least radical among us will understand that silence is no longer an option."

Greenwood's expression darkened as he tried to regain control. "Miss Foley, this is hardly—"

"Un-stop your ears, Mr. Greenwood!" she interrupted. "Perhaps if women could vote, we'd have fewer politicians like you—spineless, short-sighted, and utterly incapable of leading!"

The hall erupted into chaos. Voices clashed, feet stomped, and the din of argument filled the air. Mr. Greenwood shouted above the noise, his voice hoarse with frustration. "The courageous, chivalrous men and the womanly women are the true home builders of this nation! Keep women at home and out of politics!"

Foley's response was swift and cutting. "Women are gathering at the gates of politics, Mr. Greenwood! Hip, hip, hooray for Sibley!"

She turned and repeated the cheer three times, each call rallying more voices to join her. The moment was electric.

As pandemonium overtook the hall, Helen grabbed my arm. "Isn't she magnificent?" she said, her eyes alight with admiration.

I could only nod, too captivated to speak. Margaret Foley had single-handedly turned Greenwood's rally into a show of support for his opponent.

I watched as she slipped out through a side door, her work here done. The chaos she left behind was a testament to her power.

Helen sighed wistfully. "I simply adore her."

As for me, I wasn't sure what to make of it all. I don't know if Mr. Greenwood will win his seat in the state senate or not. I can only say that I have been forever changed.

Chapter Sixteen

THE TOWER

July 31, 1913

I WOKE up with butterflies in my stomach. Today, I turned twenty years old. It's my last birthday as a single woman—each day from now is a countdown to August 8th, the day I become Lady Gold, wife of Daniel, Lord Gold.

Not that English titles matter much in New England. I've decided I'll present myself simply as Mrs. Gold.

Daniel had planned a special day for me, starting with lunch in Little Italy. I'd developed a particular fondness for Italian food after my first encounter with pizza and was looking forward to trying eggplant parmigiana. The day would culminate in a big birthday party at our townhouse on Beacon Hill. But first, he promised me a surprise.

I couldn't imagine what it could be, but whatever it was, it required the carriage. McDoogle had it ready for us.

We set out in the morning while the July heat and humidity still lingered at a bearable level. The sun felt warm on my face, and a gentle breeze cooled my skin as we traveled down State Street. My arm was linked through Daniel's, and we sat close together, the intimacy of our connection a quiet delight.

"Where are we going?" I asked, my curiosity impossible to suppress. "You simply must tell me!"

Daniel only smiled, his eyes twinkling with mischief.

As we made our way through the bustling city, it became clear that our route would take us past the towering new construction that had become the talk of Boston. Rising from the heart of the city, the Custom House Tower dominated the skyline, an awe-inspiring sight that symbolized the city's growing modernity.

Even from blocks away, the tower was impossible to miss. Its steel girders and partially finished exterior already stood more than twice as high as any other building around it. I felt a shiver of awe as I stared at its dizzying height.

When the carriage drew closer, I gasped. The steel skeleton had climbed to 20 stories, while the finished façade reached 15. Workers moved like ants across the beams, some balancing precariously on girders high above the ground. A few even sat casually, drinking coffee as if they weren't suspended hundreds of feet in the air.

"It's like our future, Daniel," I said dreamily. "We're building our lives together, floor by floor until one day it will be complete."

Daniel's grin deepened. "Beautiful and strong."

At that moment, my love for him felt boundless.

We approached the construction site, its perimeter cordoned off by eight-foot wooden barriers. To my surprise, Daniel asked McDoogle to stop the carriage.

"What are we doing?" I asked, my curiosity piqued.

"A fellow I went to school with, Edward Greer-Brown, is one of the architects of the site. He's agreed to give us a tour."

My jaw nearly dropped. "Is that allowed? Isn't it dangerous?"

Daniel chuckled, wrapping an arm around my shoulders. "Love, I wouldn't dream of putting you in danger. Think of it as an adventure—the first of many."

The architect met us at a side gate. He greeted Daniel heartily, then turned to look at me, and his lips pursed in a soundless whistle.

"Gold, you sly dog!" he said. "You told me you're marrying an heiress to save your moldering ruin of a house; but not one word about her being a stunner!"

Daniel grinned, and I felt my cheeks warm under Mr. Greer-Brown's praise. But his teasing tone had put me at ease.

"I hope Gold proves worthy of you, Miss" Mr. Greer-Brown added with a twinkle in his eye.

"I'm sure we'll prove worthy of each other, Mr. Greer-Brown," I replied, meeting his mischievous grin with a smile of my own.

"Come along, then," he said. "I told the fellas you're potential investors, so don't let on that you know me."

He led us through the original Custom House, which had been vacated but still retained much of its historic charm. From there, we ascended to the rooftop via an old elevator.

Stepping onto the roof, I was struck by the panoramic view of the city. The North End stretched out before us, and the harbor sparkled in the morning sun. Ships dotted the water, their sails billowing in the breeze.

Mr. Greer-Brown looked at me with a pleased grin on his face. "If you think this is impressive, just wait."

He ushered us into a newly constructed elevator that served the unfinished tower.

"This lift only goes up to the fifteenth floor for now," he explained.

The ride was jerky, and my stomach seemed to lag behind as we ascended. I gripped Daniel's arm tightly, feeling both exhilarated and slightly unnerved.

When the doors opened, we stepped into a framed but unfinished space. Debris littered the floor, and the air smelled faintly of sawdust and metal.

"Watch your step," Mr. Greer-Brown cautioned. "You don't want to land on a nail."

We navigated carefully until we reached the edge of the structure. Standing there, looking out over the city, I felt a sense of wonder I couldn't put into words.

The harbor lay directly beneath us to the east, its waters shimmering in the sunlight. The Long Wharf stretched out into the distance, its orderly rows of warehouses bustling with activity. To the north, I spotted Faneuil Hall, Haymarket Square, and Copp's Hill. Turning west, I marveled at the golden dome of the State House and even caught a glimpse of our townhouse's rooftop near the Boston Common.

"This must be what it feels like to be a bird," I said softly. "From this height, it feels like anything is possible."

Daniel smiled down at me. "Happy birthday, love."

Overcome with emotion, I kissed him on the lips. "To our life's tower," I said, raising an imaginary toast.

As we descended, I reflected on the experience. Standing on the tower, I felt a mixture of awe and hope—emotions that mirrored my feelings about the life Daniel and I were building together.

When we returned to the carriage, I leaned into Daniel's side, the warmth of his presence a comfort against the day's growing heat.

This birthday was already one I would never forget.

Chapter Seventeen

MR. AND MRS. GOLD

August 10, 1913

WHEN I AWOKE THIS MORNING, I felt like I had emerged from a dream in which the bashful princess had married the handsome prince. After the prince spirited her away on a sprightly steed to their magical castle, they lived and loved furiously ever after.

Oh mercy, wouldn't Sally laugh herself silly if she ever read these words.

But for me, Mrs. Daniel Gold(!), it feels true! My handsome prince lies beside me on these silky white sheets, sleeping lightly as the day grows warmer. The sun's rays pierce through the curtains hanging from the high windows, tickling his eyelids, while the streets of Boston below awaken as if nothing spectacular—nothing earth-shifting—had ever happened.

My wedding dress hangs neatly in the wardrobe. For once, it wasn't Molly who helped me step out of my dress. I blush at the thought of Daniel's fingertips brushing the skin of my back. These thoughts—and what happened afterward—aren't suitable for recording in a journal, but the words "intensely delightful" don't quite capture the experience.

Yesterday itself started far less magical.

"Heat up the steamer," Sally barked at June, the maid. "There's a wrinkle on the back of my dress." She twisted like a stiff bread dough attempting to spot the offending crease—one I'm certain she created herself with her contortions. "Do you know how much I paid for this?"

Up until that moment, Father and I had been sharing an emotional and sentimental conversation in his study.

"After today, Daniel will be responsible for you," he said, his voice both solemn and tender. "You'll need to follow his commands, but you will always be my Ginger." His eyes shone with sentiment, and I nearly burst into tears.

"Oh, Father! I will miss you!"

"No need," he said with a faint smile. "I'm coming to London too."

The dampness on my eyelashes made them feel heavy as I blinked rapidly. "You're coming with us on our honeymoon?"

I love my father dearly, but I was quite certain Daniel and I should enjoy our wedding journey alone.

Father laughed heartily. "Your face, Ginger. Priceless."

"Father!" I exclaimed, feeling indignant. Here I was, about to be married, and he was treating me like a child.

"I'm not boarding the ship with you on Monday. My ticket is for a week later. I have business to attend to there. Pippins will have Hartigan House ready for you and Daniel when you arrive."

"Pippins?" It had been ages since I'd heard Father mention the name of our London butler. He had been so kind to me when I was a child. The thought of Hartigan House roused a flood of memories. As a little girl, I'd imagined the house as a castle, and I, at various turns, was a princess, a queen, a fairy, or even a unicorn reigning over my magical kingdom within its stone walls. I was thrilled at the thought of returning, especially with Daniel by my side.

Just then, Louisa burst through the office door, interrupting us. Sally's sharp voice followed.

"Louisa, stop being such a monkey and get upstairs to dress! Or do you want to stay home in your room while the rest of us go to the wedding?"

"But I'm the flower girl!" Louisa wailed.

I had decided to forego bridesmaids—I wanted this day to be just for Daniel and me. But of course I did have to have my little sister as a part of the celebration.

"If you don't stop fooling around we'll do without a flower girl, and we'll do just fine, I'm sure!" I heard Sally's voice as the door swung shut behind the disappearing Louisa.

Father's head dropped in silent defeat, his tired gaze staying on me. "I will miss you so very much, my love."

I walked to where he sat behind his desk and kissed the top of his head. "I'd better get dressed myself before Sally grounds me too."

Molly was waiting for me when I entered my room upstairs.

"Are you ready, miss?" she asked, her voice warm and steady.

"I am."

I sat at my vanity as Molly swept my red tresses into a neat knot at the back of my head. She then helped me into my wedding dress—a masterpiece of silk and lace, its delicate layers draping over my bodice and hips, cinched gently at the waist. The lace-trimmed veil was secured on my head, its length falling into soft, delicate pools on the floor.

Around my neck I clasped the gold locket that had

belonged to my mother, nestling the pendant into the neckline where the folds met my cleavage.

"She would be so proud of you, miss," Molly said softly.

Mother had been gone so long that, I confess, there were days I barely thought of her. But on days like today, my chest ached with longing.

"I know I'm not your ma, and no one can fill her shoes—" Molly hesitated, leaving unspoken the name of my stepmother —"but if you need a hug, I'm here for you."

"Oh, Molly." I embraced her tightly, tears seeping out from under my lids. "I'm so glad you're here."

Finally, the household was ready. Louisa was dressed, Sally's wrinkle had been smoothed—at least the one in her dress—and the carriage was prepared. Miraculously, we made it to the church on time.

The church bells of St. Aidan's Episcopal Church rang out as we arrived, their jubilant peals soaring high over the city street. A gentle breeze carried the faint scent of roses and lilies —flowers I had chosen for the ceremony.

Father extended a hand to help me out of the carriage. His warm smile was both reassuring and bittersweet. "You look stunning, my love. Daniel is a lucky man."

As we ascended the church steps, Molly bustled behind me, adjusting my veil to ensure it draped perfectly. Sally stood off to the side, fanning herself and whispering critiques to Louisa, who was bouncing on her toes with excitement, nearly spilling her basket of flower petals.

The soft strains of the organ began inside the church, and I could hear that a hush fell over the congregation. Molly gave my hand a gentle squeeze, then she slipped through the doors into the church to take her seat, and Father offered his arm. My heart thudded as I placed my hand in his, feeling the steadiness of his grip.

"Are you ready, Ginger?" he whispered.

I nodded, though the lump in my throat made it difficult to speak.

As the organist began the bridal march, the heavy oak doors swung open. Sally gave Louisa a push, and my little sister skipped over the threshold into the church, scattering flower petals ahead of her along the long aisle.

The church was a vision of serene beauty. The nave was adorned with garlands of white roses, their fragrance mingling with the faint aroma of polished wood and burning candles. The sun streamed through the stained-glass windows, casting a kaleidoscope of colors onto the polished stone floor.

But I only had eyes for Daniel. He stood at the altar, his posture upright and his expression poised, but his soft smile betrayed his anticipation. He wore a morning suit of the finest cut, the pale cravat at his throat a perfect contrast to the deep navy of his coat.

The world around me blurred as I took my first step forward. Each stride brought me closer to Daniel, his gaze never wavering from mine. The gentle murmur of the crowd, the rustling of fabric, the faint notes of the organ—all faded into the background.

Father's pace was steady, his arm a comforting anchor. When we reached the altar, he stopped and turned to me. His eyes shimmered with unshed tears as he lifted my veil, brushing a kiss against my cheek.

"Go to him," he said simply, his voice thick with emotion.

Daniel stepped forward, his hands reaching for mine. As our fingers intertwined, warmth spread through me, steadying my nerves.

The vicar began, his voice a gentle cadence that soothed the room. Though his words were beautiful, I found it difficult to focus on anything other than Daniel's face. His blue eyes sparkled, his dimple appearing faintly as he smiled.

"Do you, Daniel, take this woman, Georgia Hartigan, to be your lawfully wedded wife?"

Daniel's voice was strong and unwavering. "I do."

"And do you, Georgia, take this man, Daniel Gold, to be your lawfully wedded husband?"

For a moment, my voice caught, overwhelmed by the enormity of the moment. Then, I squeezed Daniel's hands and said with certainty, "I do."

The exchange of rings felt like the sealing of a sacred bond. The cool metal of the band slid over my finger, a tangible symbol of the vows we had spoken.

When the vicar declared us husband and wife, Daniel lifted my veil fully, his hands gentle yet firm. Time seemed to slow as he leaned in, his lips brushing mine in our first kiss as a married couple. Applause erupted around us, but it felt distant, as though we were in our own little world.

"Lady Gold," Daniel whispered against my lips, his breath warm and full of promise.

The reception was held in the gardens of the townhouse on Beacon Hill. Lanterns swayed in the breeze, and tables were draped in crisp white linens, adorned with arrangements of roses, dahlias, and hydrangeas. A string quartet played softly in the background as guests mingled, sipping champagne and nibbling on hors d'oeuvres.

Sally had spared no expense in ensuring the reception was flawless. For all her faults, she had a flair for event planning, and I couldn't deny the elegance of the affair.

Daniel and I moved through the crowd, greeting well-wishers. Many of my father's associates and their wives attended, offering warm congratulations and teasing remarks about our journey to England. Louisa flitted about, delighted to be the center of attention whenever she could steal it.

When it came time for the first dance, Daniel took my hand and led me to the middle of the lawn. The quartet began a waltz, and Daniel's arm wrapped securely around my waist as we moved together.

"You're exquisite," he murmured, his breath tickling my ear.

"You're not so bad yourself," I replied, grinning up at him.

The world seemed to fall away again, just as it had in the church. The rhythm of the waltz carried us, our steps in perfect harmony. Around us, the guests watched, their smiles warm and approving.

As the dance ended, applause filled the air, and Daniel dipped me dramatically, eliciting laughter from the crowd. When he pulled me upright, his lips brushed my temple.

"Our adventure begins," he said softly.

As the evening wore on, the laughter and joy were infectious. There were speeches and toasts, and Sally even managed to deliver a gracious, if slightly self-aggrandizing, address to the happy couple.

Father's speech, however, was the one that brought tears to my eyes.

"To my daughter, my Ginger, or rather, Georgia," he began, his voice steady but thick with emotion. "You've grown into a woman of strength, grace, and intelligence. As you begin this new chapter with Daniel, Lord Gold, know that my love and support will always be with you. And to Daniel—thank you for seeing in her what I've always known. May your lives together be as beautiful and enduring as the love you share today."

As the final lanterns flickered and the last guests departed,

Daniel and I stood hand in hand, watching the stars emerge in the night sky.

"Tired?" he asked, his tone teasing.

"Not at all," I replied, though my feet ached, and my cheeks hurt from smiling. "It's been the most perfect day."

Daniel pulled me close, his arms wrapping around me as we swayed gently to the faint strains of the quartet's last tune.

"Happy first night as Lady Gold," he said, his voice a low murmur against my hair.

I leaned into him, my heart full and content. "Happy first night, Lord Gold."

The adventure has only just begun.

Daniel awakes and his dimple deepens as he smiles at me.

"Good morning, love."

"Good morning. Should I ring for room service?"

Without answering, Daniel pulled me back under the sheets. I'm afraid this poor journal just landed unceremoniously on the floor.

Chapter Eighteen

LONDON

August 18, 1913

DANIEL and I are in London on our honeymoon! Thank goodness that dreadful trip across the sea is finally over. Daniel promised I'd get my sea legs, but by the time I did, it was too late to use them. I am just relieved to be on solid ground now, where the world no longer rocks underfoot.

Bringing Daniel to Hartigan House was an absolute thrill. It has been twelve long years since I left as a teary-faced little girl, clutching my father's hand, and yet it felt as though time had stood still here. The only notable change is that Pippins, our butler, has lost his hair—though his presence and charm are as intact as ever. The house itself is a testament to my father's care and maintenance, standing as timeless and grand as I remembered.

When Pippins opened the front door, I could barely contain my joy. Besides my father and Daniel, my childhood butler has always been one of my favorite people. I had already relayed countless stories to Daniel about Pippins and the games we used to play—I spy, Noughts and Crosses—or how he'd sneak me into the kitchen to badger Cook for tea and biscuits for impromptu tea parties.

"Welcome home, Lady Gold," Pippins said warmly, his voice as steady and dignified as ever. I blinked, taken aback by his salutation. He had always called me Miss Hartigan or Little Miss when we were alone. But I suppose that is my title now, so I will have to get used to it!

"Pips!"

Unable to resist, I threw my arms around him in an enthusiastic American-sized hug. Poor Pips reared back in shock, his staid English demeanor shattered by such an emotional outburst, but then he smiled at me. I tugged on Daniel's sleeve to make the introduction.

"Pippins, this is my husband—" I shivered with delight at the word. "Daniel, Lord Gold. Daniel, meet Pippins."

I had always thought Pippins was tall, but now, standing next to Daniel, he seemed to have shrunk. Daniel's warmth and sincerity shone as he shook Pippins' hand with enthusiasm.

"Lady Gold speaks so highly of you, Pippins," Daniel said.

Pippins' cornflower-blue eyes sparkled as a grin tugged at the corners of his mouth. "You have a very fine bride, Your Lordship."

"I do," Daniel replied with a twinkle in his eye. "Indeed!"

Eager to show Daniel everything, I led him through the house, seeing it anew through his eyes. The freshly polished black-and-white marble floors of the vast entrance gleamed, reflecting the light from the grand chandelier high above. A broad staircase curved upward to the first-floor landing, its banister smooth from years of care.

The drawing room and sitting room flanked the hall on opposite sides of the house, each furnished in late Victorian styles with heavy curtains, ornately carved furniture, and intricate wallpaper designs. Next to the sitting room was the dining room, followed by the morning room whose French doors opened onto a stone terrace that overlooked the back garden. The neatly trimmed hedges and vibrant flowers in full bloom made the air fragrant with a symphony of scents.

"Hartigan House is marvelous," Daniel said, his voice filled with genuine admiration. "Its grandeur makes Bray Manor seem even more wretched by comparison."

"Oh, Daniel," I said gently. "Things must be better now that we're married." My tone faltered slightly, knowing that Daniel's family's fortunes had hinged on our union.

"Darling, of course," he said, taking my hand. "But improvements take time. You'll see what I mean when we visit."

I looked forward to visiting Bray Manor and meeting Daniel's sister and grandmother, though I felt a touch of trepidation. From Daniel's descriptions, his grandmother sounded like a formidable woman, and his little sister a bit of a handful.

Before I could dwell too much on the upcoming visit, I had one more part of the house to show Daniel.

"Father said we could use his automobile," I said, leading him to the garage.

The double doors had been propped open in anticipation of our arrival, revealing a gleaming machine that surprised a gasp out of Daniel. Painted a deep, lustrous blue, the flat-roofed two-door vehicle features polished tires with bright yellow spokes and a rich brown leather interior that smells like newness itself.

Daniel let out a low whistle. "Is that a Daimler?"

"It is! A brand-new Daimler TE 30 Cranmore Landaulet, to be exact! Father hasn't even driven it yet," I said, beaming.

"She's a beauty," Daniel murmured, running his hand over the sleek surface.

"We'll have to take it for a drive," I said, then corrected myself with a grin. "Actually, I want to drive it."

Daniel smiled but said nothing.

The final stop on the tour was upstairs. "Our luggage should be in our room and unpacked by now," I said as we ascended the staircase.

When we reached the landing, only one bedroom door stood open, beckoning us inside. It was the room I had slept in as a child. My heart sank briefly as I imagined spending my honeymoon in a chamber decorated in soft pinks and whites, surrounded by the lifeless eyes of my childhood dolls. But as we stepped inside, my breath caught in surprise.

The room had been entirely redecorated. Gone were the pastel hues and girlish frills. In their place was a sophisticated design, neutral yet elegant, with gold and ivory furnishings and trim.

"Daniel, isn't it lovely?"

The centerpiece of the room was a large bed with an ornately carved wooden headboard and footboard. A full-length, gilded mirror stood gracefully in one corner near a matching dressing table. Two striped ivory-and-gold chairs faced the tall windows, their fabric shimmering faintly in the afternoon light.

"It's perfect," Daniel said.

I smiled, silently thanking my father. He had clearly ensured the room would be suitable for a married couple, and I felt a swell of gratitude knowing he had thought of everything.

In the far corner stood a gramophone. Daniel walked over, brows lifting as he flipped through the small stack of records next to it.

"I made a special request of your father," he said.

Curious, I watched as he selected a record, placed it on the turntable, wound the handle, and set the needle gently onto its surface. The warm crackle of static was soon replaced by the soft strains of music. I recognized the melody instantly—Frank Croxton's voice filling the air with "Road to Mandalay."

Daniel turned to me, holding out his hand. "May I have this dance, Lady Gold?"

I smiled, taking his hand. "You may, Lord Gold."

We danced slowly across the polished wooden floor, my head resting against his chest. Listening to the steady rhythm of his heartbeat, I felt a wave of contentment wash over me. This was my husband, my partner, the man I would share my life with. As the music played, I imagined the many songs we would dance to in the years ahead, the laughter we would share, and the life we would build together.

"Happy honeymoon, my love," Daniel whispered, his lips brushing my hair.

In that moment, I was certain of one thing: this was only the beginning of our grand adventure.

Chapter Nineteen

BEHIND THE WHEEL

August 24, 1913

WHAT A MARVELOUS DAY we had today! With the sun shining warmly and a gentle breeze making the late summer air delightful, I suggested to Daniel that we enjoy a picnic in the countryside.

"A perfect opportunity to take your father up on his generous offer," Daniel said, a gleam in his eye.

"And what offer is that?"

"A drive in his Daimler."

"Well then, it's settled," I said, grinning.

The cook prepared a lovely picnic basket brimming with sandwiches, fresh summer fruits, and a thermos of chilled lemonade. Daniel carried it to the car and placed it carefully in the back seat. He then moved toward the driver's side door, but before he could settle himself behind the wheel, I stepped in front of him.

"Darling," I said sweetly, "how would you feel if I drove?"

"Are you sure you know how?" he asked, raising a skeptical brow.

"Of course I'm sure! Father taught me in Boston."

"But that's entirely different," Daniel replied, concern flashing across his face. "Trust me, it's quite confusing for the uninitiated at first. We drive on the other side of the road."

"I'm sure I can manage," I said, brushing off his objections. "Besides, I'll have you to guide me!" Before my poor husband could argue further, I slid into the driver's seat, beaming with excitement.

Daniel sighed. "Very well, but let's go over a few things before we start. Your right hand operates the gear shift—it's mounted outside the body here. Your left foot controls the clutch. The foot brake is on the right, and the throttle is set by hand with this lever on the steering column. Spark advance is adjusted here too." He stepped to the front of the machine, gripped the crank handle carefully, and gave it a sharp upward pull to start the engine. Daniel jumped into the passenger seat.

"Put the gear shift in first, and carefully manipulate the clutch and throttle." He motioned with his hands what I was to do with my feet, and the motor car lurched forward. After a few jerks and grinding noises, I found the rhythm and drove out of Mallowan Court. A strangled noise came from Daniel. "The left side of the road, my dear!" he exclaimed, grabbing his hat.

"Oh, mercy! Old habits die hard," I said, laughing as I corrected my path.

Daniel kept his eyes fixed on the road ahead. "You didn't give me a chance to explain all the mechanics of driving," he said, his voice tight, then he let out another squawk as I pulled the car around a horse-drawn omnibus loaded with passengers.

"Don't worry," I said breezily, barely glancing his way. "You can tell me all about it over lunch."

"Of course. Why didn't I think of that?" he muttered under his breath, shaking his head.

He didn't say much else as we drove to the outskirts of London, although I heard him gasp a few times. The wind whipped against my face as we reached the straighter roads of Battersea and Richmond and I accelerated the vehicle, the buildings flying past and the trees of Richmond Park blurring into a tapestry of green and gold.

We reached the beginning of a hill I shifted the car into a lower gear, which was something I had observed my father do many times. There was a sudden strange grinding sound coming from underneath the vehicle somewhere as I took a moment to find the right notch, but I was sure it was nothing. The car slowed somewhat, but when I found the right gear we were off again.

"Oh, well," he said with forced cheerfulness. "The Germans build very sturdy gearboxes, I'm sure."

As we continued out into the countryside, I grew more confident, coaxing the Daimler to greater speeds.

"Is there a fire somewhere?" Daniel quipped, his voice strained.

At first, I didn't understand, but then I glanced at him and burst into laughter. His hat was clutched tightly in one hand, the other gripping the seat for dear life. His eyes were wide, his complexion pale.

"Are you feeling all right?" I asked, my laughter fading into concern.

"Oh, I'm fine," he replied, though his tone suggested other-wise. "Perhaps we could find a good spot to pull over and— watch out!"

A farmer's horse-drawn hay wagon appeared around the bend, blocking the road. The driver's eyes widened as he urged his horse forward. Without hesitation, I feathered the brake pedal, swerved deftly to the right, and eased back onto the road. We missed the wagon by at least three feet, though the rush of adrenaline made it feel much closer.

I squeezed the horn in triumph and let out a laugh. "Such fun!"

"Dear Lord!" Daniel exclaimed, his face ashen.

Not far ahead, I spotted a picturesque clearing with a walking path that led to a small stream. "Here's a good spot," I said, pulling over smoothly.

"Thanks for the lesson, Daniel," I teased as I stepped out of the car. "You taught me a lot in a short time."

"I had a few revelations myself," he said, his voice dry, as he climbed out with deliberate care.

We spread a blanket beside the stream, the soothing babble of water adding to the tranquility of the setting. The sun was warm, the shade of a nearby oak tree offering just the right amount of respite. The sandwiches were delicious, and the ripe, juicy peaches were a perfect accompaniment.

As we relaxed, Daniel lay back on the blanket, one arm propped behind his head. "I propose we take a gentler approach to our return trip," he said. "Do you mind if I drive?"

"Not at all," I replied, stretching luxuriously. "I feel wonderfully relaxed. I'd love to sit back and let the breeze wash over me while you drive." I tilted my face toward the sun, savoring the moment. "It's days like this that make one thankful to be alive."

"I would love to feel that relaxed, my love, but I fear it might take me a bit longer." He put his hat back on his head and tugged at his tie. "But yes, that pretty much sums up how I feel after that drive. Glad to be alive."

I looked at him in surprise, and then we both burst into laughter.

Chapter Twenty

BRAY MANOR

August 31, 1913

MY BREATH CAUGHT as Bray Manor came into view. Daniel had spoken of it so often and in such glowing terms that I knew it would be spectacular, yet I still found myself utterly unprepared for the sight.

The sprawling stone structure stretched between a green knoll lush with vibrant purple heather and smooth emerald-green lawns. Beyond it, a shimmering lake sparkled like a giant jewel in the summer sun.

A myriad of chimneys reached skyward from the red roof, only a very few of them showing any sign of activity—the kitchen fires, I presumed, as nobody would have a fire in the living quarters in this warm season. Hooded gables over the windows gave the manor the appearance of a slumbering giant, its watchful eyes surveying the estate.

"Oh, Daniel," I whispered, awe suffusing my voice. His lips

twitched with the hint of a smile, the kind that only comes from pride and satisfaction.

"It's quite a sight, isn't she?" he said.

"You grew up here?" I asked, still mesmerized by the sheer size of the place. Hartigan House, for all its grandeur, was no small affair, but this estate easily dwarfed it.

"Born here," Daniel replied, his voice warm with nostalgia.

No wonder Daniel had agreed to my father's arrangement —marriage in exchange for financial stability. A manor such as this would require a fortune to maintain, and if one loved it as much as Daniel clearly did, one would do anything to preserve it.

Daniel parked the Daimler and reached for my hand. He could sense my nerves.

"It'll be all right," he said, his thumb brushing over my knuckles. "Grandmama and Felicia will love you."

Would they, though? Could someone love a person they viewed as a financial savior? I resolved to do my best to put them at ease. They needed to know that my love for Daniel was real and not part of some business arrangement.

As Daniel led me up the stone path, I noticed that the closer perspective revealed signs of wear. Loose stones jutted out from the façade, vines curled untamed along the walls, and the wooden frames of the windows bore cracked, flaking paint, while the lawns, which had looked perfect and smooth from the distance, clearly could do with a trim. The grandeur was undeniable, but the estate clearly bore the weight of time and neglect.

Daniel didn't ring the bell but pushed open the grand wooden door as though he'd never been away. Of course—it was his home.

"Grandmama! Felicia!" he called, his voice echoing through the vast entrance hall.

Felicia was the first to appear. She peered down from the top of the winding staircase, her long auburn hair tied in a single braid secured with a large silk bow. She wore a soft pink cotton dress with white tights and polished satin shoes, a picture of youthful propriety.

"Daniel?" she asked hesitantly, and then her face lit up. "Daniel!"

With a shriek of joy, she flew down the stairs so quickly I feared she might tumble. In seconds, she was in his arms.

"Daniel, I missed you so much!"

Daniel kissed the top of her head, holding her close, and the sight filled my chest with warmth. I almost teared up, though a pang of guilt tugged at me. I had played a role in keeping these two apart.

Felicia glanced up from the crook of Daniel's arm and fixed me with a hard glare. Her green eyes narrowed, and her tongue darted out at me in a shocking gesture of defiance.

Such cheek!

And yet, she reminded me so much of Louisa. That awkward, pre-adolescent phase often seemed designed to test older siblings.

"Felicia, love," Daniel said, oblivious to her rudeness. "This is my wife, Georgia. She's your sister now."

Felicia pouted, her lips forming a hard line. "I don't need a sister."

Daniel bent down to her level. "But love, you've always wanted a sister."

"I changed my mind," she said petulantly. "I just want my brother."

Oh mercy, this was going worse than I'd imagined—and I hadn't even met the infamous Lady Ambrosia yet. Her arrival was heralded by the sharp clicks of her summer boots against the marble floor.

"Daniel, my dear," she greeted him warmly.

Daniel stepped forward to take his grandmother's hand and give her a kiss on the cheek, while she responded with a regal inclination of her head. She was stately, dressed in a high-necked silk blouse buttoned down the back and tucked into a long black skirt. Her hair, a mix of dark auburn and silver, was piled neatly on top of her head. She carried herself with the grace and authority of a dowager.

Then her gaze fell on me.

Lady Ambrosia assessed me with the cool precision of a horse trader appraising a new mare. Her eyes swept over my attire, pausing at the crystal brooch pinned to my bodice that I had inherited from my mother.

"Grandmama, my wife, Georgia," Daniel said, beaming. "Georgia, my grandmother, the Dowager Lady Gold."

I dipped into a polite curtsy. "Lady Gold, such a privilege to finally meet you."

"Yes, well," she replied curtly, her tone as dry as parchment. "I suppose we must get used to each other."

Turning back to Daniel, she said, "Dinner will be served at seven. That should give you enough time to settle into your room and change."

"Yes, Grandmama," Daniel replied easily, seemingly unbothered by her brusque demeanor.

The staff began to gather, curtsying and bowing as they welcomed Daniel and me home. Daniel offered warm thanks and handed the footman instructions to carry our luggage upstairs.

He glanced at his wristwatch before turning to me with a smile. "We've got some time before dinner. Would you like a quick tour of the old place?"

My nerves were still jangling from the frosty reception, but I forced a bright smile. "I'd love to."

Daniel took my hand, his grip reassuring, and led me through the grand entrance hall. I tried to focus on his warmth and the excitement in his voice as he pointed out the intricate carvings on the banisters, the imported Italian marble underfoot, and the family portraits that lined the walls.

"You'll love the library," he said, his enthusiasm contagious. "It was my sanctuary as a boy. Grandmama used to scold me for staying up late reading adventure stories by the fire."

I couldn't help but smile, imagining a young Daniel tucked away among the towering bookshelves lost in a world of daring escapades.

As we strolled through the vast corridors and sunlit rooms, I began to see Bray Manor not just as an estate but as a home—a place steeped in memories, traditions, and love. And perhaps, in time, it will feel like my home too.

Chapter Twenty-One

LIVINGSTON LAKE

September 1, 1913

THE SUNSHINE and warm breeze beckoned us to Livingston Lake, a tranquil pond more than a lake, its waters shimmering like a sapphire nestled behind Bray Manor. A dock jutted through a patch of reeds, and beside it stood a small boathouse sheltering two rowboats, their paint faded but charmingly intact. Daniel chose the rowboat painted sky blue and, with effortless strength, dislodged it from its moorings.

I admit to enjoying the sight of his strong arms, bare under the rolled-up sleeves of his linen shirt. The way his muscles flexed as he worked—it was enough to make me blush under my wide-brimmed straw hat.

"I hope you're prepared to get a little wet," he teased, his grin both playful and promising trouble.

"Is that a threat, Lord Gold?" I asked, narrowing my eyes but unable to suppress a smile.

"Only if you want it to be one, Lady Gold."

He steadied the rowboat along the dock and offered his hand to help me step in. I placed my gloved hand in his, the heat of the summer seeping through the thin fabric, and gathered my skirts with the other.

As soon as I stepped into the boat, the vessel rocked precariously, and I nearly tumbled overboard. Daniel caught me just in time, his hands firm on my waist, steadying me.

"Careful now," he said, his voice tinged with amusement.

"That was your doing," I accused, laughing despite myself.

Once I was seated, my parasol shielding me from the warm sun, Daniel climbed in and took his place at the oars. His straw boater cast a shadow over his handsome face, but the mischievous glint in his eyes was unmistakable.

The boat glided smoothly across the lake, the gentle splash of the oars mingling with the songs of birds. Reed buntings flitted out from their nests, their melodious chirping adding to the symphony of nature. A magnificent orange-beaked goose skimmed the surface of the water, its gray wings cutting through the air with grace.

"That's a greylag goose," Daniel said, nodding toward the bird. "Native to Europe, I believe."

"I've never seen one before," I said, marveling at its elegance. "At least, not that I can recall. Most of my childhood was spent in London, far from marshes and lakes."

Daniel smiled. "There's so much more to England than its cities, love."

I leaned back slightly, allowing the boat's gentle motion to lull me into a state of peace. "It's so lovely here," I said. "You must miss it terribly when you're in Boston."

Daniel's expression softened. "It's beautiful in the summer," he admitted. "But don't romanticize it too much. The winter, though shorter than what you have in Boston, is damp and gray. A place like this can feel heavy then."

I considered his words, my heart aching for Felicia and Ambrosia, who bore those winters alone. As beautiful as Bray Manor was in the sunshine, I could imagine its grandeur feeling isolating during the colder months.

Daniel rowed us toward the far side of the lake. Just beyond was a stone church, its steeple poking the sky. Behind it was a graveyard, the far end reaching the boundary of the lake. A cluster of tombstones caught my eye, their weathered surfaces standing in quiet testament to the passage of time.

"It's the family plot," Daniel explained. "My parents and grandfather are buried there. Would you mind if we stepped ashore?"

"Of course not," I said, though a shiver ran down my spine. The idea of stepping into a cemetery on such a bright, cheerful day felt incongruous, but I understood Daniel's need to visit his loved ones.

The boat rocked as Daniel steadied it against the shore. He held out his hand, and I stepped carefully onto solid ground. We walked hand in hand toward the small cemetery, the neatly tended grass soft underfoot. Whoever cared for the grounds had done a meticulous job; not a single weed marred the area, and flowers bloomed in quiet beauty around the stones.

Daniel stopped before a particularly grand tombstone. "This is Grandfather," he said, his voice reverent.

The inscription, though worn, was still legible:

> *Sir Artemis Gold*
> *November 5, 1841 – February 27, 1890*
> *Beloved Husband and Father. May He Rest in*
> *Peace.*

"He passed before I was born," Daniel said, his hand tightening slightly around mine.

We moved on to a pair of side-by-side tombstones. I already knew the story—how Daniel's parents had died in a tragic carriage accident in 1902, leaving Daniel and Felicia orphaned.

"I was eleven," Daniel said quietly, his gaze fixed on the stones. "They'd been to the opera. While the performance was on, an ice storm swept through. Their carriage collided with another and flipped into a water-filled ditch."

My heart ached for him. Without thinking, I reached for his other hand, holding both of his tightly. "I'm so sorry, Daniel," I whispered. "I can't imagine how hard that must have been for you, for Felicia, and for your grandmother."

He nodded, his jaw tightening. For a moment, we stood in silence, the weight of loss hanging between us. Then, as if shaking off a dark cloud, Daniel gently tugged me back toward the boat.

"Enough about the dead," he said, his tone lighter. "We're alive and well, aren't we?"

Before I could reply, he pushed the boat into the water and climbed in, his movements quick and sure. He rowed us back to the center of the lake, his strokes powerful and deliberate.

And then, with a wicked grin, he slapped the oar against the surface of the water, sending a refreshing spray in my direction.

I gasped, half in shock, half in delight, as the cool droplets dotted my face and arms. "Daniel!" I cried, but I couldn't help laughing along with him.

Tilting my face toward the mist, I closed my eyes and let the coolness wash over me. It was impossible to stay cross with Daniel, not when he was so full of life and joy.

As the boat drifted lazily on the sparkling water, I couldn't help but feel grateful. Grateful for this moment, for this place, and most of all, for the man who brought me here.

Chapter Twenty-Two

TEA TIME TROUBLES

November 12, 1913

DANIEL and I have settled into married life rather nicely. Our apartment near Fort Hill Square is charming, and I simply adore its view of the harbor. Watching the ships glide in and out, their sails snapping in the breeze or their smokestacks puffing trails into the sky, is a peaceful way to pass the hours.

Which, as it happens, I seem to have plenty of. With Daniel working long days alongside Father, I often find myself alone.

Daniel encourages me to fill my time with tea parties and social visits, urging me to make new friends among Boston's young society wives. I oblige him now and then, though I can't say I enjoy these gatherings.

I attended one just a few days ago and left feeling utterly dismal. My new circle of acquaintances consists of women who are either newly married, like myself, or older—shall I say— busybody types. (I can be honest here; after all, this journal is for my eyes only.) Dreadful busybodies!

"How long have you been married now, Mrs. Gold?" Mrs. Foster asked as she stirred her tea with an air of feigned innocence. Like the rest of us, she wore a ruffled high-neck blouse paired with a long velvet skirt; her ensemble topped off with a wide-brimmed hat adorned with a cluster of fake fruit.

Fruit, birds, feathers, and bows seem to be the reigning themes of hat decor these days. I wore my own simpler hat, trimmed with a ribbon and a small cluster of violets, feeling underdressed compared to the flamboyance on display.

We sat upright in our chairs, our spines rigid and barely grazing the backs, constrained as we were by the unforgiving straight corsets. One wonders why chairs for women even have backs. Truly, they're ornamental at best. We might as well sit on bar stools!

"Three months," I answered politely, taking care to keep my tone light.

Mrs. Foster exchanged a conspiratorial glance with Mrs. Long. "Ah, the honeymoon phase," she said with a knowing smile.

The ladies around the table chuckled as if privy to some grand secret. Mrs. Long's baby chose that exact moment to wail, and she began jiggling the little one on her knee in an attempt to soothe it.

"Babies are wonderful," Mrs. Long said, her eyes bright with maternal pride. "You'll never be bored again!"

The insinuation hit me like a splash of cold water. Their giggles, the shared winks—how obvious it all became. They were not-so-subtly hinting at what they believed would soon come for me: motherhood.

The thought made my cheeks burn. I wasn't "in the family way," as they so delicately put it, and their smiles only deepened my discomfort.

I raised my teacup, hoping to shield myself from further scrutiny.

Mrs. Long, her tone softening, seemed to catch my unease. "Babies come when they decide to come," she said kindly.

"Daniel says it takes time," I mumbled into my cup. "And that I shouldn't worry because I'm young."

Mrs. Long nodded sympathetically, but Mrs. Russell, ever the tactless one, chose that moment to announce, "My daughter just had her first! Little Oscar is two days old—her honeymoon baby!"

The table erupted in congratulations, but the words twisted in my stomach. Though I wanted to be gracious, a pang of envy gnawed at me. Was there something wrong with me?

Mercifully, the gathering eventually ended.

That evening, I confessed my feelings to Daniel as we sat together after supper.

"I much prefer the company of men," I told him, "where we can discuss politics or current events. I'd rather debate the situation in Europe than hear about feeding schedules and diaper strategies, let alone the difficulties in finding a good nanny."

Daniel laughed, pulling me into a warm hug. "It's why I love you, Ginger," he said, using my nickname—something he did only when we were alone and playful.

I relaxed into his arms. Though I sometimes feel isolated, I'm grateful for the suffragettes and my single friends to keep me grounded. Sally and Louisa provide occasional diversions as well, though Sally's opinions and Louisa's childish antics often leave me exasperated.

Still, I find myself worrying about Father. He took a tumble the other day with no apparent cause. The bruising on his forehead looks nasty, but it's his pride that seems most hurt.

He brushed it off when I expressed concern, laughing it away with a wave of his hand. "I'm not an old man yet, Ginger," he said. But I see the stiffness in his gait and the slight hesitation in his movements.

Sometimes, the weight of these worries feels like too much. It's strange how marriage has altered my perspective. Just a few months ago, my concerns were trivial—what hat to wear, whether Daniel would enjoy the dinner I'd planned. Now, I find myself thinking about things I can't control: babies, an aging parent, the future.

Oh mercy, this isn't a very joyous journal entry. I've always striven to write with cheer, but today, my thoughts seem heavy. Perhaps tomorrow will bring lighter spirits.

Chapter Twenty-Three

HAPPY NEW YEAR!

January 1, 1914

NOT TO BLOW my own horn, but I threw an absolute splash of a party last night! It was the kind of celebration that will surely be talked about for weeks to come. While I adore the cozy charm of my apartment near the harbor and the life Daniel and I have built there, I do sometimes miss the grand elegance of my old home on Beacon Hill.

With Father and Sally away in London, Daniel and I have had the run of the house, and last night, it was a delight to see it teeming with people again. The expansive rooms, spread over three glorious stories with their stately view of the Common, felt alive in a way they haven't for some time. Guests filled every corner, all dressed to the hilt in dazzling gowns and dapper suits, their laughter and chatter echoing through the halls.

I must confess, I felt like royalty in my shimmering blue gown. The lace bodice hugged my form elegantly, the delicate sleeves draping over my shoulders in soft waves that highlighted my slender arms. The neckline dipped modestly, just enough to showcase the embroidered lace, which blended seamlessly into layers of satin that pooled gracefully at my feet. And Daniel— oh, my Daniel—was the perfect complement. He looked striking in his dark suit with long tails, a crisp white satin bow tie, and a tall top hat. Truly, he was the most handsome man of all!

The house was abuzz with joy, the air thick with cheer and festivity. Streamers hung from the ceiling in a cascade of color, and Sally's new gramophone spun out melodies that kept the atmosphere lively. (Though I might never admit it to her, her collection of records is splendid.) When the gramophone began to play "When Irish Eyes Are Smiling", Daniel pulled me into his arms, his warm laughter mingling with mine as we danced clumsily, stepping on each other's toes.

"So long, 1913," Daniel said as the music swirled around us. "You were a very good year."

I couldn't agree more. The year 1913 was a year of milestones. It gave me my husband, took me across the Atlantic to London and back, and set Daniel and Father on a path of prosperous business ventures that sustain us so grandly.

And yet, there's something I haven't dared to voice aloud —not even to Daniel. The thought feels fragile, as though saying it might shatter it altogether. But I can write it here, quickly, before I lose my nerve.

I think I'm in the family way.

There. I've done it. My heart races just seeing the words in ink. I'm filled with hope and trepidation in equal measure, but I mustn't dwell on it. Not yet. Not until I know for certain.

Back to last night. What a night it was! Dancing, drinking, and laughter carried us through the hours. Sally, before departing for London, had been rather despondent about missing the affair and had one solemn instruction for me.

"I have a reputation in this town," she said. "It's expected that the Hartigans pull off the best New Year's celebration in Boston. I always plan fireworks on the roof at midnight. Alas, you'll have to oversee it now, Ginger."

I promised her I would, so when the clock neared midnight, I made my way to the roof to ensure everything was in place. But I wasn't alone.

"Ginger! I want to do the fireworks now!"

Poor Louisa. She'd been utterly inconsolable about being left behind when Father and Sally left for London. I'd done my best to reassure her that she'd have a wonderful time with Daniel and me, but her pouting had persisted. By the time the evening wore on, she was a wilted flower—her tired eyes drooping, her ringlets losing their bounce, and her party dress sporting a conspicuous juice stain on the front.

"I'm afraid you'll have to wait a bit longer, darling," I said gently. "Or you can go to bed."

Louisa's face crumpled into a pout, and she stamped her little patent leather boot with surprising force. "I will not go to bed."

I held out my hand. "Come and sit with me, then."

She hesitated, her lips quivering, before finally accepting my offer, and came back into the house with me. I pulled her into my lap as we settled into one of the leather armchairs in the sitting room. Louisa rested her head against my chest, her body relaxing as Daniel took the chair beside us. He looked so distinguished, his hair slicked back and his collar high around his neck.

"She's got gumption," Daniel said with a soft smile, nodding toward Louisa.

"Most definitely," I agreed, stroking her hair.

Daniel sipped his brandy and turned to me. "Are you ready for 1914?" he asked. "Does it look bright for you?"

I smiled, but before I could answer, he added, "Business looks promising, but I'm concerned about the unrest in Europe. Trouble is brewing."

"Europe is so far away," I said, hoping to reassure him. "Surely whatever is stirring across the Atlantic won't reach us here in America?"

Daniel's expression turned somber. "Let's save our serious conversations for another day," he said. "Tonight is for celebration."

I nodded, grateful to postpone such heavy topics.

When Louisa's eyelids finally fell closed, I tried to scoop her into my arms. "She's getting so big," I murmured. I didn't think I could lift her anymore.

Daniel chuckled and stood, relieving me of my burden. "I'll take her to bed," he said.

As I watched him carry her upstairs, I couldn't help but smile. He was so gentle with her.

With Louisa settled, the rest of us gathered on the roof as the clock struck midnight. The fireworks were everything Sally had promised—bright, bold, and breathtaking. Bursts of color lit up the night sky, reflecting off the Charles River. I stood with Daniel's arm around my waist, my heart swelling with hope for the year to come.

1914 will be a marvelous year. I'm sure of it.

Chapter Twenty-Four

DISAPPOINTMENT

February 27, 1914

I FEEL HOLLOW. As if a great hand reached down from the clouds and scooped out my insides, leaving dull emptiness. The hope of life I'd carried for such a short time has slipped away. It's a grief I hold alone, that can't be shared. Societal propriety doesn't allow for that.

As I go about my business, I wear a mask.

"How are you today, Mrs. Gold?"

"Fine, thank you. And you?"

Daniel knows. I didn't need to say a word. Pain tightened my face as bitter salty tears welled and flowed against my will. He held me, but I couldn't forget what I saw flash in his eyes. He too suffered pain and loss. I can't escape the feeling that somehow this is my fault.

Chapter Twenty-Five

KINGS OF EUROPE

March 16, 1914

"WHY DO the countries in England want to fight each other?"

Louisa's voice, brimming with curiosity and urgency, startled me as much as the peculiar phrasing of her question. I had just settled into my favorite chair in the sitting room of the brownstone, the Boston Sunday Globe folded in my lap, when she charged into the room, her steps full of drama.

"Countries in England?" I asked, setting the paper aside.

"I heard Father say he's worried about the countries in England fighting each other!"

"Ah, I think you mean the countries of Europe, my dear." I smiled and patted the armrest of the chair, gesturing for her to join me.

Louisa's eyes widened, her pale eyebrows raised in disbelief. "You mean England doesn't have countries?"

Suppressing a chuckle, I said, "No, sweetheart. England is a country. Europe is made up of many countries, and England is just one of them."

"Oh." She frowned, her expression crumpling into one of deep thought.

"Perhaps we should brush up on your geography lessons, hmm?" I suggested. Louisa had a knack for charming her way through school without retaining much of what was taught.

"Let's have a look," I said, crossing the room to retrieve a rolled map from Father's collection. I brought it to the dining table and unrolled it, revealing a detailed map of Europe from 1910. "Here," I said, pointing, "this is England. And here, this tiny dot is London. That's where I was born, and where Hartigan House is."

Louisa leaned in, her small nose nearly brushing the paper. "But Daniel was born there too, and he talks like Father," she said, wrinkling her nose. "I think we Americans talk more properly."

I raised an eyebrow and slipped effortlessly into my British accent. "I daresay people in England would jolly well disagree with that statement!"

Louisa giggled at my sudden transformation.

"Don't forget, dear, though you were born in Boston, Father is British. That makes you part English, too."

Her brows furrowed, and she stared at the map. "So, who are the countries that Father's afraid will fight each other?"

"That's a complicated question," I replied, tracing the map with my finger. "At the moment, tensions are rising among Austria-Hungary, Germany, and Bulgaria, as well as the Ottoman Empire. They might form one side of a conflict. On the other side, you have countries like England, France, and Russia." I pointed out each country as I spoke, giving her time to take it in.

Louisa's eyes grew wide. "Why don't they just round up all

the leaders of those countries and put them in one room together? Maybe at Hartigan House! They could have tea and biscuits and sort everything out."

The sincerity of her suggestion brought a smile to my face. "That's a very clever idea, Louisa. Perhaps if they all sat down with a good English tea, things might indeed improve. However," I added with a sigh, "it's not so simple. Many of these leaders already know each other. In fact, many of them are related."

"Related?" Louisa's jaw dropped. "They're family?"

"Yes. Let me explain. This is Great Britain," I said, pointing to England, Scotland, Wales, and Ireland on the map. "It's ruled by King George V. Over here," I pointed to Russia, "is Tsar Nicholas II, a kind of king. And here, in Germany, is Kaiser Wilhelm II. All three of these men are cousins."

Louisa's mouth formed a perfect "O."

"Queen Victoria, their grandmother, called her descendants the 'royal mob.' She had nine children and forty-two grandchildren, many of whom married into the royal families of Europe. King George and Kaiser Wilhelm are first cousins. King George and Tsar Nicholas are also first cousins, while Wilhelm and Nicholas are third cousins. And they're all fifth cousins through a common ancestor, King George II of England."

Louisa stared, utterly gobsmacked.

"Not only that," I continued, "Tsar Nicholas married Alix of Hesse, a princess from Germany who was also their cousin."

With a dramatic flourish, Louisa tipped sideways onto a chair, rolling her eyes as if the weight of royal lineage had overwhelmed her. I couldn't help but chuckle.

"Why can't they just get along, then, if they're family?" she asked, sitting upright again.

"Well," I said, raising an eyebrow, "families do have squabbles, don't they?"

She nodded solemnly, likely recalling our many sisterly rows.

"But these squabbles involve entire nations, Louisa. They're much larger and far more dangerous. Each country believes it has the right vision for the future, but when those visions clash, it creates conflict. Europe is a very small place compared to America, and there are so many languages, cultures, and histories packed into it. One nation's dream can quickly become another's nightmare."

Louisa tilted her head, absorbing my words. "Does Father think it'll lead to war?" she asked in a small voice.

I hesitated, then squeezed her hand. "Father is worried, yes. And it's wise to be concerned when tensions are rising. But you shouldn't trouble yourself with such worries, my dear. You're only ten. Your job is to focus on schoolwork, be kind, and enjoy your childhood."

Louisa nodded, though her expression remained serious.

"Now," I said with a smile, "roll up this map and put it back where it belongs. And remember, no matter what happens in Europe, you're safe here in America."

Louisa dutifully rolled the map and returned it to the drawer before bounding out of the room, her usual buoyancy restored.

I remained behind, staring at the now-empty table. How far would Europe's kings and emperors let their quarrels escalate? Would they risk dragging their nations into a conflict that could change the world forever?

The fire crackled in the hearth, warming the room and momentarily easing my concern. I turned back to my paper, determined to focus on the here and now. Whatever storms were brewing across the Atlantic, I could only hope the leaders of Europe would find a way to preserve peace. For now, life in Boston remained calm, and I was grateful for the quiet moments.

Chapter Twenty-Six

THE FIRST MOTHER'S DAY

May 10, 1914

WHEN PRESIDENT WILSON proclaimed yesterday that a special day should be set aside each year to honor mothers, my stepmother, Sally, strutted about the house as if she were the president's own mother.

"Finally, a president who understands the important contributions mothers make to society," she announced to no one in particular as we sat in the sitting room. She adjusted the lace cuffs of her high-collared blouse and tipped her head just so, a portrait of self-congratulation. "I, for one, often feel under appreciated."

I glanced around the room, half expecting Louisa to burst in, for surely that comment couldn't have been directed at me. But no, the remark was meant for me to digest—and choke on if Sally had her way.

I could have responded with a biting monologue about how she wasn't, in fact, my mother, nor had she ever treated me as a daughter—not in the way she doted on Louisa, her own flesh and blood. Or I might have pointed out that President Wilson likely had in mind the sort of mothers who worked tirelessly to nurture and provide, not those who merely relished the title while lifting nary a finger.

Instead, I took the higher road. I glanced at the mantle clock, feigned a start, and said, "Goodness, look at the time! I must prepare dinner for Daniel."

Sally shrugged with a limp wave of her hand. "Surely he can afford to hire a cook."

Of course, Daniel could afford it; he worked for Father, who paid him well. Sally knew it too.

"I'd rather do it myself," I replied lightly. "It's not so bad, you know. I think of it as art."

That earned me a smirk. Sally knew full well my cooking was closer to an experiment than an art form. I slipped away, hoping to avoid further confrontation.

So today, Sunday, May 10th, the first Mother's Day has arrived, and Sally insisted we mark the occasion with a luncheon at a charming tearoom near the harbor. She, in her high-collared blouse and large spring hat adorned with silk flowers, reminded me of a caricature of Queen Victoria— straight-backed, smiling smugly from her throne.

Father, seated beside her, looked thinner than I remembered. He works far too much. Why should he, now that he had Daniel at his side? I resolved to speak with Daniel about encouraging Father to slow down.

Our plates were delivered, and I admired my dish: baked halibut with creamy green beans. Before I could take a bite, Father raised his glass of iced tea, its silver spoon tinkling lightly against the rim. "A small toast is in order."

Sally's smile widened, and I caught the tender glance they exchanged. It startled me. I knew Father loved Sally, but I had always assumed it was a dutiful affection rather than heartfelt adoration.

"To my lovely wife," Father began, "who has stood by me all these years, but most of all, who stepped in to be a mother to Ginger and gave me Louisa."

My breath caught, and I forced a tight smile. The glance he gave me was both apologetic and pleading. We both knew Sally's mothering had been more pretended than real, yet here he was, weaving a well-intentioned fiction for the sake of harmony.

Louisa, now stretching taller with every passing week, grinned and chimed in. "When I'm a mother, I'm going to have Mother's Day every week!"

Laughter rippled around the table, though I could barely manage a polite chuckle. My throat felt tight as I smiled at Louisa, wondering what kind of mother she might become—or, painfully, what kind of mother I might never be.

"Ginger, you look like you've swallowed a bone," Sally remarked with a sharpness that cut through my reverie.

My cheeks burned. I wasn't swallowing a bone—I was swallowing grief.

Daniel's gaze was full of concern; his brows knitted as he studied me. He alone at this table knew my sorrow. Twice, I had dared to hope I might join the ranks of motherhood, only to have those hopes cruelly dashed. While Sally basked in the glory of her newfound holiday, I mourned quietly, aching for my own mother and the children I had not yet been able to bring into the world.

As the luncheon wound down, a commotion at the door drew our attention. A family entered, all lively energy: a digni-fied matron, a weary-looking husband, and a gaggle of unruly children. The mother looked at Sally, but she did not return Sally's glance with the warmth my stepmother had intended.

Sally's scowl was sharp as she muttered, "Mrs. Rothman-Bailey. She sits on the board of several charities I also serve on. She didn't see me."

"She saw you," I said under my breath. That was no oversight; it was a deliberate snub.

When the meal finally concluded, Daniel announced we would take a hansom cab home rather than ride in Father's carriage. I shot him a look of gratitude, eager to leave Sally behind for the remainder of the day.

As we stood to leave, I extended the obligatory holiday wishes. "Happy Mother's Day, Sally."

What came next utterly stunned me. Sally hugged me—an unprecedented move—and whispered two words that sent my heart racing: "I'm sorry."

Before I could respond, she bustled away, leaving me slack-jawed.

Sally, apologizing? Never in all my years had I imagined such a thing. The only explanation that came to mind was almost too incredible to consider: she knew. Somehow, Sally had guessed my struggles.

Could it be that Sally had suffered similarly? I had never wondered why Louisa was her only child, assuming it was by choice. Now, I realized how naive that assumption was. Could Sally's prickly demeanor and moments of aloofness be the scars of her own disappointments?

The thought unsettled me deeply. For the first time, I saw her not as an antagonist but as a fellow woman carrying burdens I had never acknowledged.

That night, as Daniel and I sat together in our small parlor, I confided my thoughts to him.

"Sally apologized to me today."

He raised an eyebrow. "Did she now?"

"Yes, and I think..." I hesitated. "I think she might understand what I'm going through. Maybe she's gone through it too."

Daniel set down his newspaper and took my hand. "If that's true, then you have a chance to find common ground with her. It might make things easier for both of you."

I nodded, turning the idea over in my mind. I resolved to show Sally more grace in the future. Whatever life threw my way, I would not let my disappointments turn me into someone bitter and cold. I would be kind. I would rise above.

For now, I held tightly to Daniel's hand and resolved to move forward with hope.

Chapter Twenty-Seven

THE ASSASSINATION

June 29, 1914

ARCHDUKE FRANZ FERDINAND of Austria has been assassinated.

The news will undoubtedly shake Europe to its core, but I suspect most Americans won't give the tragedy more than a passing thought. To them, it is a distant and terrible affair, one to be lamented over coffee and promptly forgotten. Few here in Boston connect the dots between this act of violence and the precarious balance of power in Europe.

But Daniel and Father are different. As we gathered for breakfast that morning, I noticed an unspoken tension between them. Later, I found them huddled in Father's office, their faces etched with worry and their voices low.

Daniel caught my concerned gaze and explained. "The Archduke and his wife, Sophia, Duchess of Hohenberg, were both killed yesterday in Sarajevo. A Bosnian nationalist pulled the trigger. The authorities detained him before he could turn the gun on himself."

I sat down, my knees suddenly weak with foreboding. I had read enough in the papers about the mounting tensions in Europe to understand that this was no ordinary assassination. "Why do you suppose he did it?" I asked, my voice unsteady.

Father waved his hand dismissively. "No need for you to trouble yourself, Ginger. This is a European matter. Your life here in Boston will remain unaffected."

I ignored his condescension and turned to Daniel, raising an expectant eyebrow.

"My wife rarely accepts a brush-off," Daniel said with a small smile.

Father sighed, lighting a cigar and puffing out a stream of smoke. "Very well," he relented. "Daniel and I were just discussing the implications of this attack. It's troubling to think about what might follow."

Daniel nodded. "The papers are calling it an act of revenge."

"Revenge?"

"Yes," Daniel said, "yesterday marked the anniversary of Serbia's defeat by Austria in 1389 at the Battle of Kosovo Polje. It was also St. Vitus's Day, a celebration for Slavic nationalists. Franz Ferdinand's visit to Sarajevo on that day was, at best, ill-advised."

Father added, "He was inspecting the imperial armed forces in Bosnia and Herzegovina—territories Austria-Hungary annexed in 1908. Many Serbians feel those regions rightfully belong to Serbia."

I nodded, recalling the simmering resentment I'd read about in the papers. "And now Austria-Hungary is blaming the Serbian government?"

"They are," Daniel said gravely. "But it's more complicated

than that. The assassin didn't act alone—there's evidence of a larger conspiracy."

"Doesn't Serbia have close ties with Russia?"

"Exactly," Daniel replied. "And Austria-Hungary is closely aligned with Germany. If these accusations escalate, it could drag their allies into the fray."

A lump formed in my stomach. "France is allied with Russia, isn't it? And Great Britain with both?"

Daniel nodded, his face grim. "If blame starts flying and alliances activate, the consequences could be catastrophic."

Father stabbed his cigar into the ashtray, extinguishing the glowing tip with unnecessary force. "It's a tinderbox over there. One spark could ignite a war."

Sally entered the room just then, her skirts rustling, and her hat tilted jauntily over one ear. "From the looks on your faces, you'd think the price of tea had doubled overnight!" She laughed at her own joke, then stopped short when no one joined in. "What's wrong?"

Father hesitated but ultimately gave her the broad strokes of the news.

Sally waved a dismissive hand. "Why on earth should we care about some random shooting in a far-off country?"

Father grimaced, and I suspected it wasn't just his aching legs causing him discomfort. "My dear, this may be more serious than you think."

"I doubt that," Sally said airily. "This will blow over soon enough. We have more pressing concerns here in Boston—such as that new mayor who clearly panders to the Irish. And his wife! Did you see her hat at the inauguration?"

"Sally," Father snapped, his voice sharp enough to make all of us startle. "I have no interest in discussing the mayor's wife's hat. This is no small matter. The actions of this assassin could set off a chain of events that changes the world as we know it."

Sally's lips pursed, but she said nothing.

Father softened his tone, leaning back in his chair with a sigh. "I'm talking about the possibility of a great and terrible war."

The room fell silent, save for the faint ticking of the grandfather clock in the corner. I glanced at Daniel, searching his face for reassurance, but even his calm demeanor seemed strained.

The implications were staggering. I thought back to the conversation I'd had with Louisa about Europe's tangled alliances and interwoven royal families. These leaders weren't just political figures—they were cousins, bound by blood as much as by treaties. Yet even that familial bond couldn't stop the rising tide of nationalism and resentment.

"Do you think it will come to that?" I asked softly.

Daniel hesitated. "I hope not," he said. "But history has shown us that hope isn't always enough."

The weight of his words settled over me like a heavy cloak.

Sally's voice broke the silence. "Well, I refuse to let the actions of a foolish, trigger-happy young man affect how I live my life."

I envied her naivety, though I knew better. The world was shifting beneath our feet, and there was no telling where it might lead.

As the men resumed their quiet discussion, I excused myself, retreating to the sitting room where Louisa was playing with her dolls. Her carefree laughter was a balm to my troubled thoughts.

"Ginger, will you help me set up a tea party?"

"Of course, darling," I said, forcing a smile.

For now, I would focus on the present, savoring the small joys of ordinary moments. But deep down, I couldn't shake the feeling that the storm was coming—and that none of us would escape it unscathed.

Chapter Twenty-Eight

BIRTHDAY TEARS

July 31, 1914

TODAY IS MY BIRTHDAY—I'VE reached the ripe old age of twenty-one—and it should have been a day filled with gaiety and celebration. Instead, it has turned into one of the darkest moments of my life, one I fear I will never forget.

I am struggling to keep my emotions under control. Equal parts anger and worry wage war within me, leaving me restless and unsettled. I am cross with Daniel for what he is now considering, but I am also furious with myself—for allowing grief and dread to shape my words so harshly.

The cause of this disquiet arrived this morning in the form of a single envelope, delivered with an air of urgency that froze the lightheartedness of the breakfast table. We had only just begun to discuss plans for the day when the post arrived. The envelope, marked with the royal seal of King George V, was addressed to The Right Honourable Lord Gold.

I had seen such correspondence only once before when

Father received a similar letter concerning trade. It had left him in a state of agitation for days. My mouth went dry as I watched Daniel break the seal, the weight of its significance already bearing down on me.

Daniel's easy demeanor tensed as he read in silence, his face betraying a gravity that made my heart sink. Without a word, he passed the letter to me.

FROM THE OFFICE of King George V, Monarch of the United Kingdom and the British Dominions, and Emperor of India.

Dear Lord Gold,

I am writing this letter to you with a heavy heart. Europe is entering a time of great uncertainty, and it is now clear to me that the peace of Europe cannot be preserved. Certain developments, particularly in Belgium—a country we have sworn to protect—have led us to believe it is time for Britain to prepare for the storm that is surely gathering.

As a member of the House of Lords, we require your presence in and support for our country at this time. I know you will be ready and willing to serve.

George R.I.

MY HANDS TREMBLED as I read. I didn't need to ask Daniel what he was thinking; I already knew. A lump formed in my throat, and my tears came fast.

"No," I whispered, shaking my head slowly. "Your place is here—with me and your family." I tried to keep my voice steady, but to my dismay, it emerged thick with emotion.

"I'm a baron," Daniel replied softly. "I'm a lord, I have a duty to my country."

I knew what he said was true but pushed back against it, my tone betraying my frustration. "You came to America to build a new life! Why can't you...?"

"Georgia, love," he said gently, "I wish I didn't have to go. And perhaps it won't be for long."

I wanted desperately to believe him, but the flicker of doubt in his eyes betrayed him. My chest tightened.

"Daniel," I said, my voice trembling with desperation, "your sense of duty and principle is unyielding, like iron. Once it's set, nothing can move it." I stopped short of calling him stubborn, knowing it would only provoke him, and it was not as if he had a choice. "But do you really think that once you see for yourself the storm King George speaks of, you'll simply board a ship and come home?"

He shook his head. "I must do what I must do. England is my homeland."

"And you are my husband," I countered. "We are of one flesh."

"Then support me in this, Georgia," he said firmly.

Tears streamed freely down my cheeks, but I made no effort to wipe them away. "And what do you expect me to do here without you? Certainly, I won't sleep. Britain could go to war at any moment!"

Daniel looked at me with a pained expression. "I understand your fear, Ginger. But aside from everything else, my grandmother and sister are in England. If conflict is imminent, they need me. I must ensure they're safe."

"Then promise me," I said, my voice breaking. "Promise..." I broke off.

He hesitated, his silence cutting deeper than words.

I stood abruptly, discarding my napkin. Without another

word, I fled to our bedroom, throwing myself onto the bed as sobs wracked my body.

I don't know how long I lay there, but the tears seemed endless. I cried for myself, for Daniel, for the life we had only just begun to build together. I cried for the uncertainty of the future and the cruel twist of fate that threatened to tear us apart.

Eventually, I felt the mattress dip beside me. Daniel lay down and wrapped his arms around me, holding me close. He didn't speak, and I was grateful for it. His silence was a balm, allowing me to weep without restraint.

When my tears finally subsided, I lay still, listening to the steady rhythm of his breathing. "I'm sorry," I whispered.

"There's nothing to apologize for," he said softly.

"But I should be stronger," I said, my voice barely audible. "I should be more supportive."

"You are strong, my love," Daniel said, pressing a kiss to my hair. "Stronger than you know. That's why I need you to trust me."

I nodded against his chest, though my heart remained heavy. I didn't trust the world nor the tides of history that seemed determined to pull us apart.

"I will write to you every day," he promised.

I clung to him, wishing I could freeze time and keep him here with me. But deep down, I knew Daniel's heart belonged not only to me but also to the homeland that had shaped him.

Chapter Twenty-Nine

THE BRITISH ARMY CALLING

September 22, 1914

TODAY BROUGHT the news I had been dreading. Ever since the formal declaration of war at the beginning of August, I had feared this moment would come. Though I was not entirely surprised, the shock ran deep, sending ripples of despair through my heart that I am still struggling to quiet.

The letter from Daniel arrived as Father and I were seated in his study, poring over the latest news from Europe. The morning papers were filled with headlines about skirmishes near the Marne, rumors of German advances, and discussions of Allied strategies. It seemed impossible to think of anything else. The war was no longer a shadowy possibility; it had become a relentless reality.

When the post arrived, I plucked out an envelope which bore Daniel's handwriting. My breath hitched, and my fingers trembled as I tore it open, desperate to see his familiar script, hoping against hope that the letter would tell me he was on his way home.

As I unfolded the pages, a photograph slipped out and fluttered to the floor. The sight of it nearly stopped my heart.

There he was, my Daniel, dressed in the uniform of a British Army lieutenant. His familiar, handsome face was now framed by the stiff lines of an officer's cap, and his broad shoulders carried the weight of his rank with a solemn dignity. My tears came instantly, unbidden and unstoppable, blurring the picture in my hands. I picked it up and pressed it to my chest before handing it to Father, who regarded it with a grim expression.

"It's like looking at a ghost," I whispered. "Or perhaps an echo of the future."

Father didn't reply, but his silence spoke volumes.

The uniform seemed foreign on Daniel, a stark contrast to the man I knew so intimately. It was difficult to reconcile this image of him, bound by duty to the whims of war, with the free-spirited, fiercely independent man I married. Somewhere in France, on some distant battlefield, a commander I would never meet could order him into danger at any moment.

I supported the cause of the war—the protection of Belgium, the defense of sovereign lands—but seeing Daniel in uniform shattered my composure. Suddenly, the war felt personal, and the distance between us became a chasm I could hardly bear to face.

"Am I being selfish?" I asked aloud, though the question was more for myself than Father.

Father placed a comforting hand on my shoulder. "You're being human, Ginger. Don't fault yourself for feeling deeply."

Later, I placed Daniel's photograph in the glass cabinet in our bedroom. Each day, I will see it and offer fervent prayers for his safety.

The letter itself was dated August 28, nearly three weeks earlier. I marveled at how long it had taken to arrive, though I knew the sheer volume of correspondence crossing the Atlantic must have overwhelmed the mail service. Father watched me with concern as I read, his cigar burning between his fingers.

August 28, 1914

My dearest Ginger,

I hope this letter finds you well and happy. I miss you terribly, and you are constantly in my thoughts. I know the news I bring will dismay you, and for that, I am deeply sorry.

I have received my commission in His Majesty's Armed Forces. As of last week, I have the rank of second lieutenant and now wear the uniform with pride. At present, I am stationed at a military training camp, though I am unable to disclose its location.

Training is rigorous—both physically and mentally—but it is necessary. We drill relentlessly in weapons handling, strategy, and discipline. Rumors abound that we will be deployed to France soon. The First Lord of the Admiralty, Winston Churchill himself, is said to be visiting soon, though nothing is certain in these times.

Men from every walk of life surround me here: clerks, factory workers, schoolmasters, and, yes, men from the nobility. Though we come from different worlds, we are united by a shared purpose—to become an invincible force for England.

Never in my life have I felt such a sense of purpose as I do now. Aside from marrying you, this already feels like the most important decision I have ever made. I don't know what the future holds, but I face it with courage, knowing I am fulfilling my duty to God, King, and Country.

Please write to me whenever you can. Communication is irregular, but the mail is flowing, albeit slowly. If you don't hear from me for weeks, do not worry. It will mean I am unable to find a quiet place to write or that the post has been disrupted.

Please, my love, try not to worry. Knowing you are safe in Boston brings me great comfort. Remember that I love you with all my heart.

Yours forever,
Daniel

By the time I finished reading, my tears had splotched the letter, blurring the ink in some places. I handed it to Father, unable to speak. He took it gently and began to read, his face betraying no emotion as he absorbed its contents.

I rose unsteadily and crossed the room to the window. The familiar view of the Boston Common stretched out before me, but instead of its usual comfort, it seemed to mock me. The Atlantic Ocean felt more vast and uncrossable than ever.

As Father finished the letter, he joined me at the window. "He's doing what he feels is right, Ginger. That's all any of us can do."

"But what if this decision puts him in harm's way?" My voice cracked under the weight of my fear.

Father placed a steadying hand on my arm. "As in all things, we must have faith."

I nodded, though my heart was far from convinced. That night, as I placed the letter beside Daniel's photograph in the glass cabinet, I whispered a silent prayer:

Please, Lord, bring him back to me.

Chapter Thirty

NEW PLANS

October 15, 1914

I'VE NOT BEEN SLEEPING WELL. TOSSING and turning, assaulted by my thoughts. What am I doing? What am I doing here? The Battle of Ypres began three days ago. Is Daniel all right? He's so far away. A war rages in Europe, and my only concern is which dress to wear with which hat? Never have I felt so useless.

Then it dawned on me. I will go there! Not to France, obviously, but to England. There, I can actually be of some help with the war effort. How funny that I fell into a deep, peaceful sleep almost immediately after making that decision.

However, when I announced my intentions the next morning at breakfast, it was as if I had set off a bomb.

"Absolutely not," my father said, slamming his half-empty coffee cup on the table, its contents sloshing over the rim. "War is no place for a woman."

I scowled at him. "But—"

Sally interrupted, her expression taut and smug. "Don't be so ridiculous, Ginger. I thought you, of all people, had more sense than that."

Louisa mimicked her mother, pursing her lips in an exaggerated way that made my teeth grind. Flinging a ringlet over her shoulder she said, "Don't be ridiculous, Ginger."

"I'm not being ridiculous," I said through gritted teeth. "I'm being sensible." I turned my focus back to my father. "I have family there now, Father. Daniel's aging grandmother and his young sister. They're losing the manpower they depend on to the army." I placed a hand on his sleeve and dialed up my British accent. "Surely you can understand this? What kind of wife am I if I don't step in to watch out for Daniel's family whilst he fights for his country?"

Father's shoulders slumped, his breath escaping slowly, a sigh of defeat. "Ginger..."

"But who would look out for you?" Sally demanded. "Don't you see what you're doing to your father? Such a venture is the epitome of recklessness."

Father raised a palm, silencing her. "Sally, she's right. She's my daughter—"

I noticed again how I was always his daughter and not their daughter, even when coming from his own lips. It used to cut deeply, but somehow it didn't sting the way it once had. Perhaps because, for the first time, I felt like I truly belonged to myself.

"—but she's Daniel's wife," Father continued. "And his family is in need of her presence and comfort more than we are."

"Thank you, Father," I said, immensely relieved. I would've hated to battle with him for his blessing and permission, and even though I know I would've found a way to go without it, I was grateful it hadn't come to that.

"I will not get in your way of doing what you think is right," he said, "but I do ask that you postpone your trip until after the holidays. Once you're gone, we do not know when you'll return. Please allow us to have that time with you."

I swallowed. Waiting for the holidays to pass meant waiting over two months. Each day would be an agony of impatience and thumb twiddling. I wanted to protest—to insist I leave at once—but I caught myself before I spoke. There was a lot to get in order, after all. I needed to shop and pack and prepare goods to bring along to Bray Manor. I could write to the dowager and ask what specific needs they had, and two months might be what it would take to get a letter there and back, with the slow way the post moved these days. Perhaps time would move more quickly after all.

"Very well, Father," I said. "I'll book my passage for the first of January."

At last, I felt a twinge of appetite. I cut into the bacon and eggs that had cooled on my plate and took a bite. Now that Father and I had an agreement, I found I didn't care that my food wasn't hot. I got enough heat from the glare Sally directed at me from across the table. I sipped my tea, averted my gaze, and changed the subject. "So, what's the latest from the society news? Anything of interest?"

Sally sniffed and turned her nose up. "As if you care about society news."

"Oh, but I do," I said sweetly. "You must keep me informed, or however shall I know which salons are still worth attending?"

Louisa giggled, clearly enjoying the exchange, but a sharp look from her mother silenced her.

Father cleared his throat. "I received a letter from the Pembrokes. Their son George enlisted when Daniel did."

I looked up sharply. George Pembroke. He is a mate of

Daniel's. We met when Daniel and I went to London for our wedding journey. He is polite, a good conversationalist, and has that easy, effortless charm that some men possess. But now he is off to war. Will I ever see him again? Will anyone? The thought was, and still is, unsettling.

I drew in a breath. "That's why we must do what we can to support the war effort." I let my gaze rest on Sally. "Even from this side of the pond."

Sally let out a long sigh, apparently resigned to my decision. "At the very least, don't go embarrassing us when you get there."

I laughed, the tension breaking at last. "Oh, Sally, I shall be the very model of propriety."

Father chuckled. "That'll be the day."

I smiled into my breakfast tea, knowing full well that propriety had never been my strong suit. And, if I was being honest, I didn't intend to start now.

Chapter Thirty-One

BACK IN ENGLAND

January 7, 1915

I DESPISE TRAVELING across the Atlantic, especially in the middle of winter! It seemed as if we hit one squall after another. My stomach couldn't hold down a bit of food, and my legs felt like overcooked pasta noodles. My kind companions on the ship tried to encourage me, "You'll get you sea legs yet!" Unfortunately, six days at sea wasn't long enough to accomplish that feat.

By the time I got to Liverpool, I wanted to kiss the ground, though my legs were still so wobbly I feared I would fall over and not be able to right myself once more.

The train trip from Liverpool to Hertfordshire took another two days, so I chose to break my journey in Coventry. The misery of the transatlantic leg of my travels did produce one good thing in that I slept like the dead, and if the hotel's chambermaid had not knocked on my door as vigorously as she did to wake me and kept on knocking, I would have missed my connection for the next part of the journey.

I hired a carriage to take me the last part of the way from the train station. When Bray Manor came into view, I almost didn't recognize it beneath the dark gray clouds. The lawns were a sad, depressed color that trended towards mud, and no purple dotted the hills. Of all the chimneys that sprouted from the red tiled roof, not many more than the previous summer showed a plume of smoke. The windows that once looked like watchful eyes, now were dim and closed, as if the manor was hibernating for winter. I could hear Daniel's voice from two years previous when we'd visited on our wedding journey. "A place like this can feel heavy during the long winters."

The driver carried my trunks and suitcases to the front door while I tapped the large brass knocker. I wondered if anyone would answer. Ambrosia had responded to my letter telling her I was coming, though I hadn't been able to give her an exact date and time. I grabbed the scarf around my neck, tightening it against the winter wind, wondering if I might have to locate another hotel, when, after a third knock, the door squeaked open.

The butler standing before me was older than the hills. Shoulders hunched, eyes watery, gray hair greased back, he walked with a cane! No wonder it took ages for him to answer the door.

He peered at me suspiciously through rheumy eyes. "How can I help you?" His tone clearly indicated that he had no expectation whatsoever of being able to actually do so.

"I'm Mrs.... er... Lady Gold, the Dowager's granddaughter by marriage. I believe you were ill the summer Lord Gold and I were here."

Bushy brows pinched over his nose. "Granddaughter? Oh,

yes, her ladyship did mention she expected you. But I was not told it was today."

Laboriously, he pulled the door open wider, and I gratefully stepped in out of the cold, though it wasn't exactly warm in the entry way. I motioned for the carriage driver to bring my luggage inside, then tipped him well. When he was gone, I glanced at the pile and then at the butler.

"Is there a footman, uh...?" I asked.

"Sheffield, my lady. Yes, young Robert. I will have him take your luggage up. . The Dowager is in the sitting room."

I followed Sheffield, knowing where he was headed since I'd been here before.

"Lady Gold, my lady," Sheffield announced, opening the door of the sitting room.

The Dowager sat upright in a plush, wood-trimmed wing-back chair, which had been pushed close to the fireplace. Though the thick drapes were opened, the room remained dark with only a few lamps fighting against the gloom. The dancing flames of the fireplace reflected in the manner of a kaleidoscope off the glass of the many framed paintings hanging on busy wall-papered walls.

A young woman relined on a matching settee, a book propped on her lap. It took me a few moments to recognize her as Felicia! Though not much older than Louisa, Felicia had matured much faster. Even though she still wore the shorter skirts of girlhood and had not yet put up her hair, she was beginning to show decided curves, and her prominent cheekbones promised that before long she would be a beauty.

I resisted the urge to curtsey. "Lady Gold," I said. "I hope I'm not intruding."

Ambrosia rose to her feet, and after a sharp glance at her granddaughter, Felicia rose too.

"Of course not," Ambrosia said. "You are family, so naturally, you're always welcome. It wasn't clear from your correspondence when you would arrive. I hope your travels were uneventful."

"Quite all right," I lied.

A middle-aged parlour maid came into the room. "My lady, you rang?"

"My granddaughter-in-law has arrived. Please bring tea and something to eat and tell Mrs. Tinsdale to include her in the meal considerations. I believe her room has been readied for some time?"

"Yes, my lady," said the woman with a curtsey, and disappeared.

Ambrosia sat, motioning for me to take a seat in an empty armchair. I wished I hadn't surrendered my warm wool coat to Sheffield when I came in; in spite of the fire the room felt glacial.

"We're down to two men indoors, and Mrs. Tindale and two maids," Ambrosia said. "Other than Langley, of course." The shadows under her eyes didn't move with the light, indicating they were a permanent fixture. Her hair was grayer than it was the last time I saw her, but she'd lost none of her dignified grace.

Felicia scoffed. "Sheffield and Robert are hardly men."

"Felicia!" Her grandmother sent her an icy stare. "You will mind your manners."

"Well, it's true. Sheffield is a great-grandfather and Robert doesn't even shave."

"How are you, Felicia?" I asked, hoping to diffuse the tension.

The girl huffed. "I will die an old maid. All the real men are being slaughtered. But I'm too young to do anything to help. I'm bored out of my mind."

"You are a child," Ambrosia said. "And you have no business thinking of men at your time of life."

I got the feeling the Dowager Lady Gold had run out of the energy needed to challenge Felicia's contempt.

"It's difficult, I know," I commiserated. "Perhaps while I'm here, we can make ourselves useful together."

The tea arrived, and the conversation turned to the war.

"The newspaper arrives twice a day," Ambrosia started, "and I immediately read the names of those in our town and area who've been lost, then thank the heavens when Daniel's name isn't mentioned."

"Surely they deliver news to the families before posting announcements in the paper?" I asked.

Ambrosia nodded. "One would hope."

"Alice said that she heard that Kaiser Wilhelm approves the bombing of Britain," Felicia said. "But not London, so that he doesn't accidentally kill his relatives in the royal family."

Ambrosia gave her a sharp look. "Whatever do you mean, 'bombing'?"

"Airships," Felicia said. She seemed to take a certain pleasure in her knowledge. "You know, Grandmama, they're like floating balloons with a railway carriage attached underneath. And they're talking of dropping explosives from them, bombs."

"On people? And buildings?" the Dowager said, incredulous. "Surely not!"

I shook my head. "I'm afraid I read the same thing this morning in the paper I picked up at the station."

"Good Lord," Ambrosia muttered.

We three women had one massive worry in common, and that was Daniel, the last of the Gold family line, in constant peril.

"If Daniel doesn't come back," Felicia blustered, "I'll kill him."

"Young lady!" Ambrosia said.

"I'll hold him down," I said. Ambrosia and Felicia stared at me, and the room grew quiet. I almost blurted out an apology, but then Felicia started laughing. "You're funny, Georgia."

"These days, we retire early to save on lamp oil," Ambrosia said, changing the subject. Her face tightened as if the words pained her to speak them. I imagined that a lady accustomed to the ease and comforts of life wouldn't enjoy making concessions.

The early supper was simple, but tasty, and I was surprised to hear that most of what went into it had come from no farther away than the village. There were no exotic delicacies here, as shipping goods from the continent was impossible.

"If we had known to expect you today," the Dowager said a little stiffly, spooning a potato out of her soup, "we would have had something more appropriate."

"This is perfectly appropriate," I said, "and delicious. Please don't do anything different because I am here." I speared a piece of ham.

Ambrosia thawed visibly. "Mrs. Tindale will be glad to hear it. She has been—well, out of sorts."

"Her grandson has gone and enlisted," Felicia said. "Gerald. He's only sixteen."

"I thought eighteen was the minimum age," I said.

"They lie," Felicia said, a note of despair in her voice. "So many of them lie, each eager to do their bit, you know."

True to her word, after supper Ambrosia declared it was time for us to retire to our rooms. Felicia led me, oil lamp in hand, up the stairwell—the temperature notably cooler than in the sitting room, which had doubled as the dining room—to the same room Daniel and I had stayed in previously. My mind immediately placed him there, lounging casually on the bed, his hair mussed, and his nightshirt unbuttoned at the neck. He patted the empty spot beside him. *Come to bed, darling.*

"Ginger? Are you all right?"

Felicia's voice snapped me out of my reverie.

"I'm fine. Just tired." As the words left my mouth, I realized they were true. A wave of exhaustion threatened to take me off my feet.

"Robert lit the fire," Felicia said. "It's his final job each day before he leaves for home to help his own mother."

"I appreciate the warmth."

"It won't last. Wood is cut and stacked..." She pointed to the wood holder near the hearth. "If you need to stoke it during the night. Grandmama and I are sharing a bed—" she made a face "—it helps to keep us both warmer, but I still have to get up at least once to add wood to the fire."

"Thank you, Felicia."

"Good night, Ginger." Felicia skipped out of the room. Despite her childlike way of dressing it was all too obvious that she was being forced to grow up much too soon.

I readied myself for bed, feeling glad that I had come and wondering how I can help. The last thing I want is to be a guest who needs taking care of. No, I am going to roll up my sleeves, like these other Gold ladies, and finally, finally, do my bit.

Chapter Thirty-Two

LIFE AT BRAY MANOR

January 21, 1915

THESE LAST TWO weeks at Bray Manor have felt both like two months and two days. The days are cold and long, yet somehow, at the same time, the weeks pass quickly. One wakes up on Monday morning and, before one realizes it, it's time to go to bed on Friday night.

War is serious business here. Not a single person forgets, even for a moment, that a war is raging just over the Channel. Each day, weary bodies are dragged from chore to chore.

Ambrosia spends her days knitting—scarves, gloves, socks —for all the soldiers on the front. I believe she secretly hopes Daniel will be a recipient, and perhaps, in her mind, she sees all the soldiers as Daniel. Every few minutes, when she thinks no one is watching, she pauses to rub her knuckles, grimacing as she tries to ease the pain in her hands caused by every purl and stitch.

Felicia tries to follow her example, and she sits next to her

146

grandmother, her tongue protruding from the corner of her mouth as she produces countless snakes of lumpy scarves that are more to be praised for the good intention of their maker than her craft. But at least she makes an effort.

I know myself to be useless with a pair of knitting needles, but I had brought rolls of fabric at Ambrosia's request and, of my own volition, a box of cookies and candies. Handing out treats to hardworking children fills my heart with joy. The fabric has gone to the sewing circle of ladies who worked long hours creating uniforms for soldiers. My contribution allowed them to sew new clothes for their own children, who often ran about in threadbare garments.

Today, I borrowed the manor's horse and carriage to go into Chesterton and assist the sewing ladies. Ambrosia can boast of owning a motorcar, but there is no fuel available to run it.

Sheffield shuffled to the door to open it for me when he saw me about to leave. His nose was red from the cold, and he looked like he would benefit from a knitted scarf himself—not that he would wear one in the house in the course of his duty, it being against a butler's dignity.

"Have a safe drive, my lady," he said.

"Thank you, Sheffield."

I had bundled up, wearing several layers and heavy wool blankets over my legs, but, as always, I arrived at the parish hall damp and cold. The small town of Chesterton seemed deserted in a disconcerting way, with most of the able-bodied men having enlisted as soon as the war broke out. The streets were muddy and empty except for a tired-looking horse between the shafts of a delivery van parked in front of the post office and a few housewives doing the last bit of shopping for their tea.

The musty smell of the church hall made my nose twitch, but I pushed the unpleasantness aside and closed the door behind me. The small cast iron stove in the corner of the room gave off a faint heat, but it barely pushed back the damp chill of the afternoon. Three women sat around a wooden table, their fingers busy with needles and thread, the plain fabric pooled in their laps like rippling water.

"Lady Gold!" Mrs. Hayworth's voice held both relief and exhaustion as she rose, brushing a hand over her apron. "You're a godsend, truly."

I smiled and set the parcel down on the table, untying the twine with deliberate care. The women leaned in, their eyes widening as I unfolded yards of dark wool, sturdy cotton, spools of thread, and skeins of wool. I had brought enough to last for a few months but didn't want to overwhelm the ladies by delivering it all at once.

"As I said, it's the least I could do. And I'll bring more next week."

Mrs. Hayworth touched the fabric as if it were silk from the Orient. "All this thread—it's an answer to prayer. We were nearly out. How on earth are we meant to sew without thread?"

She gestured to a pile of half-finished tunics. "I don't know how we're supposed to keep up when there's barely anything left to work with."

Across the table, Miss Edith Price, a thin, sharp-featured woman, shook her head, her mouth tight. "And the worst of it is that what we send off doesn't always reach them," she said, stabbing her needle into a sleeve seam. "I heard from my cousin in France—her package was returned, waterlogged and ruined. It never made it to the front."

"Perhaps the Red Cross will ensure these get through," I offered gently. "I can make inquiries."

Miss Price exhaled, nodding, though doubt lingered in her eyes.

Beside her, Mrs. Dorothy Fields, who must have been nearing sixty, shifted in her chair and rubbed her stiff fingers. "If only these old hands could work faster," she murmured. "But the cold's got into them, and I can't keep up. My Arthur used to chop firewood, but now it's just me, and I have to choose—heat the house or finish the knitting."

Mrs. Hayworth let out a breath and resumed her stitching. "We're all stretched thin. I've got no one to mind the shop when I'm here, but what choice do we have? They need warm blankets, tunics, and bandages, and they won't sew themselves."

I sat down beside her and picked up a spool of thread, threading a needle. When I had first arrived with a buggy full of supplies, they had nearly refused to let me help. My lady, no. My lady, we couldn't. I had to insist, and only because of my title—the very thing that had stood in the way—they relented.

I found that my sense of fashion lent itself well to quickly learning the finer skills required for making and following patterns and sewing them by hand.

Mrs. Fields gave me a small smile. "You do have a way of making things seem less grim, Lady Gold. And we are thankful for that."

The fire crackled. My needle slipped through fabric, stitch after careful stitch.

Your country needs you.

We answered the call—one seam, one thread, one shared burden at a time.

Chapter Thirty-Three

VOLUNTARY AID DETACHMENTS

February 15, 1915

My head is spinning!

Today felt like one of those pivotal moments that alters the course of a life forever. I began the morning with a clear plan: return to Boston. My train ticket to Liverpool was practically arranged, and the next logical step would be to book a ship across the Atlantic, for which I needed to go to London. The idea of being back in Father's brownstone, with familiar sights and comforts, seemed like the most desirable course of action. But by the day's end, everything had changed.

The journey from Bray Manor to King's Cross Station was filled with thoughts about the future. I was grateful for every moment I'd had with Daniel's family, but as the distance from Bray Manor grew, so did the heavy feeling of separation. The idea of leaving England now, of putting an ocean between Daniel and me, suddenly felt unbearable.

England is alive with purpose. The air hums with the kind

of energy that can only come when an entire nation is united toward a singular goal. Everywhere you look, people are answering the call to action, contributing to the war effort in whatever way they can. It's inspiring and humbling, too.

Boston, by comparison, feels so far removed, so insulated from the reality of what's happening here. I understood now why Daniel had felt compelled to come here, and to stay. How could I ignore the same call, knowing that he is here, facing unimaginable challenges? The thought of returning to America and simply praying from afar was more than I could bear.

By the time I arrived at King's Cross, my resolve had completely shifted. Instead of heading to the travel agent, I walked with purpose to the nearest Red Cross station and requested to speak with the person in charge of volunteer enlistment.

That's how I found myself face-to-face with Mrs. Wallace-Chamberlin. A woman of imposing presence, she had the sharp eyes of someone who missed nothing, and an air of no-nonsense efficiency. Though dressed in civilian clothes, her manner was that of a military officer.

"I'm one of the people in charge of enlisting volunteers for our Voluntary Aid Detachments," she explained briskly.

"I've heard of them," I replied, "but I'm afraid I don't know much about what they do."

She regarded me for a moment, then leaned forward. "The VADs provide vital support to naval and military forces. We're organized under the Joint War Committee, often working under the Red Cross name for legal protection and to safeguard our workers in the field. Our work spans nursing, transport, organizing rest stations, and more recently, supporting communications."

Her explanation only deepened my curiosity.

"If you're truly interested in joining, I'll need to know more about your background," she said, picking up a pencil and poised to take notes.

I eagerly shared details of my education, focusing on my arithmetic and sciences, though she seemed most interested when I mentioned my fluency in French.

"Do I detect an American accent?" she asked, her pencil pausing mid-word.

"Yes," I admitted. "I was born in London, but I've lived in Boston since I was eight."

"Married?" she asked, her gaze flicking to the ring on my finger.

"Yes, to Lieutenant Daniel Gold. He's serving in France now. In civilian life, he is Baron Gold."

Her eyes narrowed slightly, not with suspicion but curiosity. "That makes you Lady Gold."

"It does," I said cautiously. "Is that a problem?"

"Not at all," she replied, though her tone suggested it wasn't the answer she'd expected. She set her pencil down and laced her fingers together.

"Let me ask you this: do you consider yourself a good communicator?"

"I believe so," I said confidently.

"Organized?"

"Reasonably. I wouldn't call myself disorganized."

"Do you get frustrated easily?"

"Certainly not."

She studied me carefully over the rim of her spectacles. "If a man were rude to you on a telephone line, could you maintain your composure and focus on the matter at hand?"

I blinked, momentarily puzzled by the question. "I believe I could, yes. Especially if the situation were important enough."

"Have you ever seen a telephone switchboard?"

"I must confess I haven't," I admitted, feeling a bit sheepish.

She nodded knowingly. "The Americans are leading the way in electrical communications, and we've adopted much of their innovation. Across France, we've laid hundreds of miles of telephone lines, all connected through switchboards. Operating one is no small task."

Her words piqued my interest.

"Switchboard operators are a critical link in the chain of command," she continued. "They field calls from generals, soldiers, and even civilians, often acting as translators for conversations between English and French speakers. It's demanding work that requires precision, focus, and a calm demeanor. Frankly, I believe women are better suited to the role than men."

"I can see why," I said, intrigued.

She tapped her pencil against the edge of her desk. "I'm inclined to recommend you for aptitude testing. If you pass, you'll be sent to a training unit in the south of England and eventually deployed to France."

Her words sent a thrill through me, but she wasn't finished.

"Be aware, Lady Gold, that once you are deployed, you will not be able to share your location or specific duties with anyone—not even your husband."

The weight of her words settled on me. This was no small commitment, but I knew in my heart that it was the right path.

I left the Red Cross station with my mind racing. As the train carried me back to Bray Manor, I couldn't help but feel that my life had shifted irrevocably. This decision was not just about supporting the war effort; it was about standing by Daniel, even from a distance, and contributing to a cause greater than myself. I feel like I'm about to dive off of a very high diving board, uncertain if there is water in the little bucket below. I have set my foot on an unknown and profoundly life-changing path.

I'm still wondering about how I'm going to tell Daniel that I won't be going back to America. He might try to talk me out of staying or even worse, forbid me to take the tests. I'm going to have to give it some thought before I write to him.

I hope I can sleep tonight.

Chapter Thirty-Four

THE SWITCHBOARD

May 7, 1915

IT FEELS as though the last few months have flown by at breakneck speed. So much has happened that I can barely recount it all, and I'm afraid my poor journal has suffered from neglect. I will try to capture the most significant details here, though I must omit certain sensitive information. Should this journal ever fall into the wrong hands, I cannot risk disclosing any names, places, or operations that might aid the enemy. Some secrets must remain untold.

Completing my VAD training in a small town in the south of England, I found myself surprisingly adept at one particular part of the work. Our instructor referred to it as having a "natural knack" for switchboard operations and rapid communication. The expectation was to connect calls in under ten seconds —a standard of efficiency we were reminded of constantly. I never imagined I'd possess such a skill, but somehow, under the intense pressure of training, my hands seemed to move with an instinct I hadn't known I had. So it was quickly decided that I was best suited to that work, rather than going into nursing as most of the other women were.

The training was rigorous, a constant dance of darting hands and non-stop chatter. The room buzzed with energy as we plugged wires and connected calls, and snippets of conversation in English and French flew about. Men and women trained side by side, though as the days wore on, fewer and fewer men remained. Many dropped out, finding the demands of the work overwhelming, while others were disqualified. It quickly became evident that my recruiter had been right—women seemed naturally suited to this role. Perhaps we can juggle multiple conversations better than men, or perhaps it is our capacity for patience under pressure, but whatever the reason, some of us excel.

The journey to my current station was fraught with more excitement than I care to repeat. Crossing the English Channel was supposed to be a straightforward affair, but fate had other plans. A thick fog descended as we neared the French coast, making it impossible for our ferry to dock. The captain had no choice but to anchor three miles offshore. There we remained, bobbing on the open sea for two long days. The fog provided some cover from German ships, but we were told that one in four ferries crossing the channel had been struck by enemy fire. It was a sobering statistic, and though the threat was ever-present, there was little to do but wait.

Sleep was a luxury I could scarcely afford. Curled up on the open deck with my head resting on a life preserver, I managed only brief snatches of rest under a thin blanket. The air was damp, the deck cold, and my thoughts restless. Every creak of the ship and every distant sound of aircraft set my nerves on edge. When the fog finally lifted, we wasted no time racing to shore at full speed. I shudder to think how close we came to disaster, but perhaps that same fog that delayed us also saved us.

From the port, we traveled inland by train, a journey that lasted nearly a full day. The countryside blurred past, a patchwork of fields and villages that seemed so peaceful compared to the chaos we knew lay ahead. When we arrived at our station—a small village I cannot name—we found it understaffed and in disrepair. Though far from the front, the strain of the war was evident everywhere. The station was barely functioning, with insufficient workers to handle the volume of calls or maintain the premises. Without hesitation, we rolled up our sleeves and got to work cleaning, organizing, and making minor repairs.

I was one of only five women among fifteen newly arrived recruits. The rest were men, most of whom were visibly relieved to have us there. I took over a switchboard from a young man whose rudimentary French had made the work nearly impossible for him. His gratitude was palpable, and it spurred me to tackle my new responsibilities with determination.

I sat down in front of the board and greeted the young woman sitting at the switchboard beside me. She was a very serious-looking woman about the same age as me, with brunette hair and fierce-looking brown eyes.

"*Bonjour, mademoiselle*, my name is Ginger," I said in French, deciding nicknames would be better than legal names in this situation.

"Ginger—*comme l'épice, gingembre?*"

"Ah, no. Not like the spice." I chuckled, one hand moving self-consciously to my head. "It is an English nickname for persons with my color of hair."

"My name is Marianne." Her smile was quick and to the point, just like her general demeanor seemed to be. She extended a hand. "I've been here for two weeks already. It's good to see they are bringing more women to help. Are you ready for this?"

"*Oui*," I said simply. This wasn't a time for chit chat.

The first call I handled was from a general in Paris. He was connecting with a squadron leader to give the go-ahead for a mission. My fingers moved swiftly over the board, connecting the lines in the required ten seconds. My heart raced as I listened to the calm, commanding voices of men making decisions that would shape the course of the war.

The second call was far less dramatic—a soldier near the front asking for the correct time. It was a small request, but I sensed the strain in his voice. Even mundane questions carried the weight of a man far from home, clinging to small comforts.

The third call was one of the most fascinating. A French operator connected me to a leader of an underground network operating behind German lines. He needed to communicate with a British supply sergeant who spoke no French. Acting as translator, I relayed the network leader's list of desperately needed supplies—ammunition, medical kits, and tools for sabotage.

The interaction felt surreal, knowing that the man on the other end of the line was operating in constant danger. He risked his life daily to disrupt enemy movements, gather intelligence, and aid Allied forces. His voice, calm yet tinged with urgency, painted a vivid picture of the high stakes he faced. It wasn't lost on me that even a stray noise overheard on his end of the line could betray his location.

My fourth call was from a French soldier attempting to reach a medical unit. His English was broken, but I assured him I could help translate. His voice wavered as he described the dire need for medical supplies for his comrades. He thanked me profusely, comparing my voice to that of his sister. His words brought a lump to my throat, and I had to compose myself before finishing the call.

The fifth call shook me to my core. A battalion leader at the front was trying to reach a general in Paris for permission to retreat. His voice, trembling with urgency, described the unrelenting bombardment his men were enduring and the heavy losses they had suffered. He mentioned his own injury—a rifle wound to the shoulder—and I could hear the chaos of gunfire and shouting in the background. When the general denied his request and ordered them to hold their position, the weight of that command felt crushing, even from the safety of my station.

Each call brings a new glimpse into the enormity of this war. I feel as though I am connected by wires to the lives and struggles of so many. Every voice I hear carries the weight of hope, despair, and determination. Though I am far from the front, I know my work matters. This war is being fought not only with weapons but with words and connections.

I'm in the thick of it now.

Chapter Thirty-Five

AN UNUSUAL ENCOUNTER

May 21, 1915

I HAD the most unusual encounter last night. A group of us girls working the switchboards often go to Bar du Bassett, a tavern frequented by both the French and British, for a drink to unwind after a long day. As it turned out, it was only me and Celine who braved the stormy weather that had rolled in, huddling under a shared umbrella as we approached the ancient stone building. The sharp wind threatened to wrench it from our hands, and by the time we stepped inside, the hem of my skirt was damp from the puddles.

The tavern always smells of tobacco smoke, body odor, and cheap wine but it only takes a few minutes before one's sense of smell becomes inured, and one stops noticing.

Last night, the dim light from flickering wall sconces gave the impression of stepping into a medieval fortress. Rough wooden beams framed the ceiling, and the air hummed with loud conversations in both French and English, overlapping into a chaotic symphony. The tavern was nearly full despite the weather, with soldiers in varied states of inebriation chatting loudly, glasses of frothy beer spilling over the rims of their glasses. Certain pretty girls in frilly dresses lounged provocatively against the bar, laughing with men who appeared far more invested in the company than the ale.

Though we were in France and far from the German zone, the absence of enemy soldiers created an illusion of safety and merrymaking. One could almost pretend that there wasn't a war raging just beyond the horizon.

Celine and I claimed an empty table near the back. "Those girls, laughing all the time, make our work feel like drudgery, don't they?" Celine said, casting a disdainful glance at the bar. "I sometimes wonder if we're in the right business."

She said it in jest, I think, but after twelve hours of sitting in front of a switchboard, my back was frightfully sore. I laughed despite myself. "I don't think I could stand their sort of work either."

We ordered our ale, and as we waited, I briefly caught the eye of a British soldier, older than us by at least a decade, seated in the corner behind Celine. He quickly looked away, giving the impression he hoped he hadn't been caught staring. I preferred that to the type who refused to glance away, believing a long look would arouse some kind of attraction. I was always careful to wear my wedding ring, purposefully going without gloves to ensure no misunderstanding.

Just as our ales arrived, a dark-haired French soldier with a thick mustache and round spectacles stumbled past our table, nearly knocking over my drink. He removed his cap and stared me in the eye. *"Je suis désolé, mademoiselle!"*

I answered back in flawless French, "It's *madame*, and it's quite all right." Thankfully, the soldier continued without further intrusion.

The drunken soldier's interruption caused the British officer in the corner to glance my way again. My heart gave a strange jolt as recognition dawned. Though we'd never been formally introduced, I'd seen him about town and, on occasion, in the building where I worked. But why was he behaving so oddly?

Before I could puzzle over it, my attention was captured by the sudden eruption of a quarrel between two French soldiers near the bar. One of them was the drunken soldier whom I'd just talked to.

"I was talking to her first, Fournier!"

"Lambert you are a liar!"

They glared at each other, their fists clenched, ready to throw punches. The young brunette who had been their focus backed away, her face pale with fear. The men's voices grew louder, and I knew the situation could turn ugly very quickly.

Without thinking, I stood and approached them, slipping between the two men before they could act. "*Arrête!*" My voice was firm and authoritative.

The soldiers froze, their fury momentarily replaced by confusion. They stared at me as though I'd dropped out of the sky. I forced a smile and batted my eyelashes, determined to diffuse their alcohol-infused rage with a dose of feminine charm. "Gentlemen, please, you are better than this." Placing a hand on each of their arms, I cooed, "You're heroes of the French army! You're on the same side. Heroes!"

The word struck a chord. Slowly, the tension in their shoulders relaxed. I continued, my voice soft and placating. "Thank you for your service, Monsieur Fournier. And you, Monsieur Lambert. You both make your country proud."

War could make a man feel worthless—worthless enough to fight over a call girl. All they needed was a reminder that the opposite was true.

Monsieur Fournier's lips twitched, forming a crooked grin. Monsieur Lambert chuckled, shaking his head. Within minutes, their feud was forgotten. Backs were patted, and Fournier called on the barkeep to refill their drinks.

As I turned to return to my table, feeling, I admit, rather proud of myself, I was intercepted by the British officer from the corner.

"What you just did was impressive," he said.

I shrugged off the praise. "It was nothing."

"Not true, madame. You may have prevented an outright brawl."

He extended a palm. "I'm Captain Smithwick."

I shook his hand politely, all the while calculating how I could step away without being rude. As I averted my gaze, I noticed Fournier watching Captain Smithwick with narrowed eyes. Smithwick caught his gaze, and something passed between them—a subtle, unspoken exchange. Before I could register its significance, the captain posed a question.

"May I buy you a drink, Mrs. Gold?"

I stilled. He knew my name.

"I'm with a friend," I said cautiously.

"Of course. Then perhaps we could meet another time. I have a proposition for you—on behalf of The Crown."

His voice was low and gravelly, war-hardened by years of command and perhaps a few too many cigars. "Skills like you just displayed are precisely what we need. Someone who can read people well... and influence them."

I now understood why I'd seen the captain about so frequently. He'd been watching me. Without his spelling it out, I knew what he was proposing. My heart raced, pounding hard in my ears. What I said next could change everything—the whole direction of my life. My future, and Daniel's, could be determined by my answer. It was a course, once started, that could never be reversed. A thread, once knotted, that could never be untied.

It was an opportunity for me to do something more substantial for the cause than simply manning a switchboard day in and day out.

I stared Captain Smithwick in the eyes and, with the utmost assuredness, said, "Yes. I'll meet with you."

Chapter Thirty-Six

SPY TRAINING

June 1, 1915

I'VE BECOME convinced that if I'm to continue documenting my experiences, I must use a substitution cipher. It would be far too dangerous—for myself and those around me—if this little book were to fall into the wrong hands.

Starting with this entry, I will be using my own code. Interestingly, I began developing this particular cipher purely for fun when I was thirteen years old. Looking back now, I can't help but wonder if there was some kind of divine plan for my life. After all, what thirteen-year-old girl spends her time creating codes instead of practicing the piano or reading novels?

Thankfully, the cipher is still firmly embedded in my memory. I've refined it using techniques they've begun to teach here, and I'm confident that it's now truly impenetrable. When all of this is over, it may take me some time to translate everything back into plain English, but I believe it will be worth the effort, even if no one ever reads it. In any case, I've come to understand that writing my thoughts down has become my way of managing the stress and complexity of these extraordinary days.

And now I will continue.

One never knows which way the wind will blow! Two weeks ago, I believed my service to my country was tied to a long panel of switchboards sitting in a row with other quick-minded operators. But here I am, just a fortnight later, a student at a spy school! It still feels unreal.

The training takes place in an unassuming, presumed-abandoned hotel outside of a village in northwestern France. It's a sleepy little town with cobbled streets, the sort of place where life moves unhurriedly—quite the contrast to the covert, frenetic pace of what we are learning inside its walls.

There are eight recruits: six men and two women. I must be purposefully vague; I can't disclose the exact whereabouts or the name of the village. However, I can say the view from my second-story room, which I share with my roommate, is breathtaking. The rooftops of the village below glisten in the morning sun, and the rolling countryside is dotted with wildflowers in full bloom.

My roommate is a lively, clever girl from Newcastle. For the purpose of this recording, I shall call her Jane, though that isn't her real name. She has a sharp wit and a way of lifting spirits, even after the grueling intensity of our lessons. We've become fast friends, and I feel incredibly fortunate to have her as my comrade during these challenging days.

The time of year is simply wonderful. The warm breezes and cheerful sunlight make it hard to believe the world is at war. The beauty outside is a stark contrast to what we are preparing for within: the art of deception and survival.

I've discovered that nothing here is as it seems. For

instance, the quarrel at Bar du Bassett—the one between those two French soldiers—was entirely staged for my benefit! Officer Fournier, as I'd known him (though that's not his real name), orchestrated the entire scene to test my instincts. Since then, I've spotted him once, sans spectacles, conversing intently with Captain Smithwick. He hasn't approached me, and I doubt he ever will.

It's all part of the lesson: trust no one and question everything.

Since arriving, I've been trained to handle firearms, including a German Luger 9mm and the British Webley Mark V. I much prefer the Luger; it's lighter and easier to handle. We've also learned how to decipher coded messages, write invisible ink letters, pick locks, and even create escape plans using maps etched into tiny fragments of rice paper. Then there's the physical training: learning how to disarm an enemy, deliver a precise blow, and even flip a grown man onto his back with the right leverage.

Yesterday, I practiced scaling a wall using nothing but a grappling hook and my wits. My arms ached terribly afterward, but I made it to the top faster than any of the men! The instructor smiled approvingly and said, "Perhaps the ladies will be the better spies after all."

We've also been issued new identity cards. I am now officially Antoinette LaFleur, a Frenchwoman by birth. My accent is still a work in progress; apparently, a faint British-American lilt sneaks into my French. Tomorrow, I will work one-on-one with a language expert to perfect my speech. A single slip could cost me my life if I'm caught behind enemy lines.

The most difficult part of all this is the secrecy. Daniel can never know about my training or my new role. The thought of deceiving him twists my heart into knots. How I long to write him a letter and pour out all my fears and triumphs! Instead, I must craft vague, cheerful missives that reveal nothing of my true activities.

Jane, too, has a sweetheart serving somewhere in France. We've spent many evenings musing about the possibility of our men crossing paths. Perhaps they're fighting side by side even now, unaware that their women are training together, preparing to step into danger themselves. We've made a pact: after the war is over, the four of us will reunite in London and celebrate over a fine meal at a French restaurant. Jane insists she'll have us all in stitches with tales of our exploits.

Laughter has become a precious commodity. In these heavy days, moments of joy feel like stolen treasures.

A tap at the door interrupted my writing. Jane entered, her face alight with excitement.

"We're going shopping. For clothes!"

"Clothes?" I sat my pen down, intrigued.

"They're getting us ready for our first assignments," she said, switching to French. "Antoinette, it's time to build your wardrobe."

The sound of my new name sent a shiver down my spine—part thrill, part trepidation.

"I hope we'll be assigned together," I said.

A shadow passed behind Jane's eyes. "That would be nice," she said softly. "But I wouldn't count on it. Let's just enjoy the time we have together."

"Yes, we shall," I agreed. "As far as training goes, shopping is something I know well!"

We laughed as we descended the stone stairwell, our voices echoing like music through the old building. I didn't take our good humor for granted. This could very well be the last moment of joy we share before the theater of war swallows us whole.

Chapter Thirty-Seven

FIRST ASSIGNMENT

June 30, 1915

I'M UTTERLY EXHAUSTED! Each morning, we recruits are awakened at dawn for rigorous calisthenics before being fed a simple breakfast and launched into another grueling day of instruction. Every aspect of our training is designed to strip away any notions of comfort or complacency, preparing us for a life where quick thinking and decisive action will mean the difference between survival and death. My pulse races at the thought of what lies ahead.

A month after starting, I'm on my first assignment. The transformation has been startling. I am no longer Georgia Gold, or Ginger for that matter. That identity, while not forgotten, is tucked safely away in the folds of memory. As Mademoiselle Antoinette LaFleur, I'm the only child of François and Marie LaFleur of Toulouse. My fictional parents are, sadly, deceased, and I've created a plausible backstory that explains my presence here. Antoinette has a beloved cousin,

Gisèle, whom she has traveled to meet at the quaint Hotel Durand in a small village in occupied North-Eastern France. The ruse is simple yet effective, allowing me to linger without arousing suspicion.

The Hotel Durand itself is charming in its rusticity, a family-run establishment nestled in a pastoral setting not far from a bustling railway line. I've noticed that many of its patrons are transient, staying only a night or two before continuing their journeys. This suits my cover story perfectly. Antoinette is awaiting her cousin, and in the meantime, she's enchanted by the idyllic surroundings.

Some of the prettiest hotels I've ever seen are here in France. I mentioned this sentiment to the French concierge upon my arrival, speaking in the most effervescent tone I could muster, with hands flailing in exaggerated animation. *"Ooo! Cet hôtel est tellement pittoresque!"*

My enthusiasm earned glances from the French and German soldiers lounging in the foyer. Their gazes lingered just long enough to confirm that they were intrigued, but not suspicious.

That's right, gentlemen. This lady is far too simple to be a dangerous spy.

At least I can confirm that my French is in top shape. No one has questioned my accent thus far, a testament to the linguistics training I received under Captain Smithwick's meticulous instruction. I've worked tirelessly to shed any trace of my American and British inflections, and it seems my efforts have paid off.

My room at the Hotel Durand is small but comfortable, with a single bed, a modest wardrobe, and a window that offers a clear view of the railway tracks behind the building. This view is crucial to my mission. My assignment is to observe the trains passing through and, more importantly, to identify a specific German train scheduled to make a brief stop here. The train, I've been told, will be transporting supplies to the frontlines. My task is to determine the nature of those supplies: are they artillery, medical equipment, or something else entirely? The information I gather could be vital to our war effort.

As I began to unpack my few belongings, a knock at the door startled me. Standing in the corridor was a young woman, perhaps my age, with warm eyes and an air of brisk competence.

"Bonjour," she said. "I am Julia Durand. We're pleased to have you as our guest. Is there anything you require?"

"Not at the moment," I replied. "Might I assume this is your family's hotel?"

"It is," she confirmed, her smile fading slightly. Glancing down the hallway, she lowered her voice. "Though only for as long as the Boche allow it."

Her candor caught me off guard, though I quickly masked my reaction. "Indeed," I said, my tone measured. "For now." I extended a hand. "Antoinette LaFleur. It's a pleasure to meet you."

"The pleasure is mine, Mademoiselle LaFleur," she replied, shaking my hand. Then, leaning slightly closer, she asked, "May I inquire as to the purpose of your stay? It helps us better attend to our guests' needs."

The question set me on edge. Was she merely being hospitable, or was there a more insidious motive? One could never be too cautious in times like these. Still, I managed a bright smile.

"I'm here to meet my cousin," I explained. "She should arrive before the end of the week."

Julia's smile faltered slightly. Was it disappointment? Suspicion? Or simply fatigue? "I hope you enjoy your time in our village," she said. "If you'd like, I can recommend some lovely places for dining and evening walks. Just be mindful of the curfews."

"Thank you. I'll keep that in mind."

Her gaze flickered toward the window overlooking the railway. "I'm sorry about the noise from the trains," she said. "But one does get used to it. They don't run all day, at least."

My heart skipped a beat. Did she suspect something? Or was I being paranoid? Either way, I couldn't let my guard down. One wrong word, one careless action, and my entire mission could be compromised.

"Noise doesn't bother me," I said breezily. "I'm sure I'll sleep soundly."

Julia hesitated for a moment, then offered a polite nod and excused herself. As the door clicked shut, I let out a slow, steadying breath. I'd passed the first test, but I knew there would be many more to come. For now, I needed to focus on my task: blend in, observe, and gather as much information as possible.

It's a strange thing, living a lie. I've practiced my new identity until it feels almost real, but there's always a part of me that wants to cry out, "I'm not Antoinette LaFleur! I'm Ginger Gold, an American from Boston!" Yet I can't afford such indulgences. To succeed in this role, I must fully become Antoinette, even in my own mind.

As I sit here writing by the soft light of a single candle, the room is quiet save for the occasional whistle of a distant train. Tomorrow, I'll begin my surveillance in earnest. The weight of this responsibility is immense, but I'm ready. At least, I hope I am.

Chapter Thirty-Eight

JULIA

July 5th, 1915

MADEMOISELLE JULIA DURAND doesn't know who I really am, and she never will.

Our unexpected friendship has been the biggest surprise of this mission so far. Every morning, the lovely Julia knocks on my door with an invitation to join her for tea and cupcakes on a cozy rooftop balcony overlooking the train tracks. Beyond the tracks stretch fields and forests, their greenery soothing in contrast to the tension that pervades our lives. Sparrows chirp cheerfully nearby, darting among the ivy that clings to the walls, as the sunshine bathes us in warmth. If it rains, we shelter under a large umbrella, giggling at the dampness that occasionally seeps through.

Around Julia, I'm somehow able to relax in a way I hadn't thought possible. I can be...myself, or at least the version of myself that Antoinette LaFleur represents. It's a peculiar paradox: sharing genuine moments of joy while living under a false identity.

Have I enjoyed myself a little too much on this mission?

Yesterday morning, as we sipped our tea, Julia leaned back in her chair, brushing a strand of hair from her face. "Your cousin still hasn't arrived, has she?" she asked, her tone gentle but curious.

I felt a pang of guilt so sharp it nearly made me wince. Lying to a stranger is one thing; lying to someone who feels like a friend is quite another. Of course, there was no cousin. My gaze flitted to the train tracks. Those two parallel lines of steel that vanished into the horizon had brought me invaluable intelligence on German troop movements and supplies—information I'd scrawled on scraps of paper and covertly hidden in the hollow cylinder handle of my plain black umbrella.

"I... I just hope nothing awful has happened to her," I stammered, my voice catching slightly. I quickly forced a smile and caught Julia's gaze, not wanting to appear evasive. "It seems everything these days is so unpredictable. I haven't heard from her yet, so I'm not sure how much longer I can wait."

Julia reached across the table and patted my hand sympathetically. "I'm sure she's fine, Antoinette. Things have a way of working themselves out."

Later that evening, as I lay in bed, I stared at the ceiling, Julia's words echoing in my mind. Do things work themselves out? This war has been anything but predictable. Over the past few days, I'd eavesdropped on snippets of conversation between German soldiers stationed at the hotel and the nearby restaurant, inserting myself into situations with calculated charm. Convincing them I was nothing more than a harmless, flighty French girl was a delicate dance, one I executed with feigned simplicity and subtle cunning.

But I sensed an undercurrent of preparation as I listened—

a quiet but palpable buzz among the Boche. Something was happening. Something big.

Early this morning, I was jolted awake by the distant yet unmistakable sound of a train. *Chuga-chuga-chuga-chuga*. I leapt from bed, a rush of excitement coursing through me, and scurried to the window, careful to conceal myself behind the curtain's edge.

The train slowed...slowed...then came to a full stop just beyond the station. My breath hitched as I watched a German soldier jump from one of the freight cars, a flashlight in hand despite the glow of the hotel's exterior lights. One by one, more soldiers disembarked from the passenger cars further along the track. I began counting them, my heart pounding with each addition. Thirty in all, each carrying rifles slung over their shoulders.

A commanding officer—likely a sergeant, though I couldn't see his insignia clearly—began barking orders. Moments later, three small motor transport trucks arrived, their engines rumbling softly in the pre-dawn quiet. The soldiers swung open the freight car doors and began unloading heavy wooden crates, stacking them efficiently onto the trucks.

This was the moment I'd been waiting for. My mission had always been clear: observe, document, and report German troop movements and supply logistics.

Moving quickly but silently, I took out a pencil and scribbled the details onto a scrap of paper. The crates, the number of soldiers, the vehicles—all of it. Once finished, I carefully rolled the note and slid it into the hollow handle of my umbrella, my hands trembling slightly. I dressed quickly and headed downstairs, ostensibly in search of an early breakfast.

In the dim light of the hotel lobby, I placed my umbrella in the communal stand, where it would be collected by an unseen ally. Minutes later, as I lingered in the kitchen, sipping tea and making idle conversation with the cook, I noticed my umbrella had been replaced. The switch had been made.

Back in my room, I retrieved the new umbrella, locking the door behind me. My fingers fumbled as I unscrewed the handle, revealing a rolled-up note inside.

Get out IMMEDIATELY. Don't speak to anyone.

A chill swept through me. The message was terse, its urgency unmistakable.

Who had sent it? Captain Smithwick? Someone else within our network? It didn't matter. What mattered was that my cover had been compromised.

My thoughts immediately turned to Julia. Sweet, unsuspecting Julia, who had no idea who I really was or the danger that now surrounded us both. I whispered a quiet goodbye under my breath, a lump forming in my throat. I wished I could have told her in person, thanked her for her kindness, her companionship, her laughter.

There was no time for sentiment. Grabbing my small bag, I stuffed it with essentials—clothing, a few francs, and my journal. Within minutes, I was slipping out the back of the hotel, the early morning shadows cloaking my movements.

I didn't look back. I couldn't afford to.

Chapter Thirty-Nine

THE CAPTAIN

July 6, 1915

I'M in a safe place now, though I'm still trembling from the events of this morning.

I'd hurried to the station to catch the next train back to headquarters. The urgency of the note left no room for deliberation, though I couldn't help but wonder who had sent it—and why. Those questions would have to wait. My priority was simple: cross into unoccupied France by 1300 hours.

The streets were eerily quiet as I walked to the station. Only the sound of my hurried steps broke the silence, but my heart hammered so loudly it seemed to echo off the cobblestones. The twenty-minute walk felt like an eternity, and when I turned the final corner, my stomach dropped.

A group of five young German soldiers lounged in front of the station entrance, laughing and smoking cigarettes, their pot-shaped *Pickelhauben* with their pointy spikes in the center perched on their heads. I've had numerous encounters with

German soldiers during my brief time in this village, and though I've grown somewhat accustomed to their presence, this felt different. The way their laughter abruptly ceased when they noticed me, the way their eyes followed my every step—it sent a shiver down my spine.

One of them, a brash-looking teenager with closely cropped blond hair and an insolent smile, blocked the entrance with one booted foot.

I paused, gripping my suitcase tightly. "*Excusez-moi, s'il vous plaît*," I said, forcing a polite smile.

The blond soldier, whom one of his companions later called Armin, took a long, slow drag on his cigarette, exhaling the smoke lazily. His blue eyes glinted with a mix of amusement and curiosity.

"You look like you are in too much of a hurry, *Fräulein*," he said in broken French.

"I wish I wasn't," I replied, keeping my tone light but steady. "My cousin has taken very ill in Charmes. I must go to her at once. We are very close, you see."

"Ah, that is too bad," he said, his voice devoid of sympathy. "My colleagues and I have just arrived here, and I feel sad that you will not join us tonight at the Hotel Durand for drinks." His eyebrows rose suggestively. "Don't you think you could stay just a little while longer?"

Another soldier, a larger man with a thick neck and a cruel smile, chimed in with even worse French. "I agree with Armin. She should stay."

My blood ran cold as the others nodded, their grins predatory.

"I'm afraid I can't do that," I said firmly, meeting Armin's gaze without flinching. "My cousin is seriously ill. She may even be dying."

The playful light in his eyes dimmed slightly as he studied

me. For a long, tense moment, he didn't move. Then, slowly, he shifted his boot, clearing the way.

"*Merci*," I said, my voice steady despite the racing of my heart. I walked past them with measured steps, resisting the urge to break into a run.

As I approached the ticket counter, I overheard one of the soldiers mutter in German, "*Zum Teufel, warum hast du sie gehen lassen?*" Why the devil did you let her go?

I didn't care why he had relented. I was just grateful he had.

But my relief was short-lived. After purchasing my ticket, I felt a sharp tug on my suitcase. Whipping around, I saw the larger soldier standing behind me, his expression dark. Armin and the others were close on his heels, their demeanor more menacing than before.

I was surrounded.

"Please, I..." I stammered, my voice trembling. My mind raced, searching for a way out. The station was nearly empty, and the few bystanders avoided my gaze, unwilling—or perhaps too afraid—to intervene.

"*Meine Hübsche*," Armin said with a smirk. My pretty. "My friends have convinced me that—"

"*Was ist hier los?*" A sharp, commanding voice cut through the tension like a blade.

The soldiers snapped to attention, dropping their cigarettes to the cobbles where they smoldered softly, as a man in a captain's uniform strode toward us, his expression thunderous. He was of medium build, with brown hair partially hidden beneath his cap, and his brown eyes radiated authority.

"What's going on here?" he demanded again in German, his voice crisp and cold.

Armin hesitated before replying, his eyes fixed straight ahead. "*Nichts*, Herr Hauptmann Krantz. We were only asking this *Fräulein* if she would join us for drinks later."

The captain turned to me, his tone softening. "Is this true, mademoiselle? I see you have a ticket. Are you catching a train?" His French was far better than the others'.

"Yes, I am," I said, mustering my composure. "I must get to Charmes. My cousin is gravely ill." I forced a small smile. "I think it would be lovely to join these gentlemen another time, but unfortunately, I cannot."

Captain Krantz studied me for a moment, then with a rapid movement turned to the soldiers.

"Abtreten, Marsch!" he barked. Stand down, now.

The soldiers' salutes clanged against the rims of their pointy helmets.

"Jawohl, Herr Hauptmann!" they snapped out in unison, and in perfect rhythm their boots thudded off down the platform.

Turning back to me, Captain Krantz said, "I apologize for their behavior, mademoiselle. They are young and far from home. Most of them haven't seen the front yet, and their immaturity shows."

I nodded, though his explanation did little to ease my lingering unease.

"Allow me to escort you to your train," he offered, extending his elbow.

Reluctantly, I accepted, walking arm in arm with the German captain. The irony was not lost on me. Here I was, a British spy in disguise, being protected by the very enemy I was working against.

As we reached the platform, the whistle of my train sounded in the distance. The captain released my arm and stepped back. "Safe travels, mademoiselle," he said with a small nod.

"Merci, Hauptmann Krantz," I replied, my voice steady but my thoughts swirling.

As the train pulled into the station, I climbed aboard and found a seat near the window. I watched as Captain Krantz walked away, his posture rigid and his expression unreadable.

Once the train began to move, I leaned back in my seat and let out a long, shaky breath. My hands still trembled as I clutched my bag.

Hauptmann Krantz. I will remember that name.

Chapter Forty

BEAUVAIS, FRANCE

September 10, 1915

NOT LONG AGO, Warsaw fell to Austro-Hungarian and German troops, ending over a century of Russian control over the city. The news left us all feeling deeply anxious about the tide of the war on the Eastern front. Now Bulgaria has announced its alliance with the German side, intending to invade Serbia. Any hopes for an early end to this conflict seem to be slipping away with every new report.

As always, my thoughts drift to Daniel. Where is he tonight? Is he safe? Is he thinking of me now, as I am of him?

Last night, I undertook what I can only describe as the most desperate gamble of my life. It's the kind of thing that makes your pulse race and your palms sweat long after the event has passed. In order to save the life of a person who is prominent in the movement to resist the German occupation —whom I'll call CV—I had to drive from a small town just across the line of German demarcation through an enemy checkpoint.

CV, the head of a substantial spy ring, had been caught past curfew alongside a British operative. The two of them were leaving a clandestine meeting when they were stopped by two German soldiers. Suspicion grew rapidly, and sensing the danger, CV acted first. He managed to disarm the soldiers with a quick draw of his revolver.

The pair took the disarmed soldiers to a nearby bar cellar, a safe house run by members of the movement. But the situation deteriorated when one of the soldiers revealed a trench knife that had been overlooked during the initial confrontation. A violent struggle ensued, resulting in the death of both Germans. In the chaos, CV sustained a serious stab wound to his chest, which narrowly missed his lung.

Despite the chaos and danger, the resistors worked swiftly. They arranged for an automobile equipped with a hidden cargo space, and I was summoned to smuggle CV across the line. My qualifications—fluency in both French and conversational German, and the ability to drive—made me the logical choice.

It's astonishing how much contraband a seemingly empty-headed, gossiping French girl with fluttering eyelashes can smuggle past German guards. All it takes is a vapid expression, convincing papers, and an air of nonchalance. Though I played the part well, my stomach churned with anxiety the entire time.

Once safely past the checkpoint, I helped CV out of the hidden compartment and into the passenger seat. His blood loss was alarming, and I knew I had to act quickly if he were to survive. I pushed the little French-made Peugeot to its mechanical limits, speeding through the countryside under the pale light of the moon.

CV, pale and sweating, gripped the dashboard with his free hand and alternated between vague responses to my attempts at conversation and exasperated exclamations like, "*Mon Dieu, femme,* watch out for that pothole!" and "*Bon sang*! I will die on this road before I reach the triage!"

It would have been humorous if it hadn't been for the dire circumstances.

After an interminable hour of white-knuckled driving in the dead of night, we reached the triage unit. By then, CV was only semi-conscious, his breathing shallow. American medics rushed to carry him to the operating table, but as they moved him, one muttered, "The doctor in charge is away on another emergency."

I couldn't believe my ears. "I just risked my life to save this man, and now you tell me the doctor is out?"

A calm, confident voice interrupted. "I can help him."

The voice belonged to a nurse, an American, judging by her accent. She wore the crisp white uniform of her profession, her dark curls pinned neatly back. Her square face was attractive in an unconventional way, but what struck me most was her take-charge manner.

"I'm Nurse Haley Higgins," she said. "I've assisted on operations like this before. Please stand back—or better yet, wash your hands if you're staying."

There was no way I was leaving. Determined to see CV through to the end, I rolled up my sleeves and scrubbed my hands.

Nurse Higgins didn't disappoint. With practiced precision, she stemmed the bleeding, stitched the wound, and dressed it, effectively saving CV's life. I assisted where I could, holding instruments and swabbing blood as directed.

"Nice work," I said afterward, maintaining my French persona. "I'm Antoinette LaFleur, by the way."

"Thank you," Nurse Higgins replied, her tone modest. "For the compliment and your help. Care for a coffee?"

I followed her to a small gas ring where a pot of overcooked coffee sat simmering. It was quite possibly the worst coffee I've ever tasted, but I drank it gratefully, feeling the warmth spread through me.

"You're full of surprises, Mademoiselle LaFleur," Nurse Higgins said, her dark eyes assessing me over the rim of her cup. "I'd never have guessed you had what it takes to dupe the Germans and rescue one of our own."

I smiled wryly. "I could say the same for you. You're more skilled—and might I say, more intelligent—than many of the egotistical doctors I've encountered."

She sighed, her expression softening. "We women will always be underestimated."

Her Bostonian accent caught my attention. I masked my unease with casual curiosity. "You're from America. What part?"

She seemed to relax, sipping her coffee before replying. "Boston. And you are French?"

"From Toulouse," I said smoothly.

I sipped my coffee, keeping the butterflies of unease at bay. Boston was a large city. I was quite certain I'd never met Miss Higgin's before, but the Hartigan family was rather well known in social circles.

I glanced at Nurse Higgin, her dark eyes staring at nothing as her mind worked. Her countenance was poised, yet unassuming. I relaxed. Miss Higgins was the type to spend her free time reading medical journals, not the social pages in the local rags.

This morning, just as I was readying to drive back, a parcel was handed to me. Inside was CV's German-made Böker trench knife, along with a note from Nurse Higgins.

. . .

Dear Mademoiselle LaFleur,

Our soldier awoke with profound gratitude and admiration for your bravery. He insisted that I find a way to give you this knife as a token of thanks. I suggest you refrain from keeping it on your person.

With respect,
  Haley Higgins

I LAUGHED ALOUD. Imagine me, a British spy in disguise, carrying a German trench knife across France! Nurse Higgins' advice was wise. I will send the knife to London straight away before I report back to my superiors.

Chapter Forty-One

COCO CHANEL

October 14, 1915

MY SECRET IDENTITY was in real danger of being exposed today. Here I am, in German-occupied France, where a single slip could mean my imprisonment—or worse. If my true identity had been uncovered, not only my life but countless others would have been at risk.

Sometimes, one's past can become one's enemy.

I had just finished meeting with members of the Réseau de renseignement local (Local Intelligence Cell) or RRL, for short. The subject was the smuggling of a nine-year-old boy out of occupied territory, through unoccupied France, and eventually across the channel to England. The boy had lost his parents and sister to the Boche and had been wandering the countryside alone for a week, starving and scared. An elderly farmer had taken him in, caring for him as best he could, but the farmer's health was failing, and he decided the boy would be safer with relatives in England.

The RRL had arranged for the boy to be transported to a hospital that served as an underground relay station. From there, a network of operatives would guide him to safety. My task was to act as the boy's mother until I could hand him over to the right people.

We were seated in the hotel bar, discussing the logistics of the plan. The room smelled faintly of cigarettes and brandy, and I kept my voice low, careful not to draw attention to our conversation. As I sipped a glass of wine, I became aware of a woman across the room who was watching me intently.

She was dark-haired, fashionably dressed, and seated with a young Frenchman in a tailored suit. They were chatting over glasses of wine, but her gaze landed on me far too often for comfort. I deliberately avoided looking at her, but her interest in me was unsettling. I had purposefully dressed plainly—no adornments, just a simple dress meant to blend in. My red hair was the only thing that might draw attention, and I cursed it silently.

After some time, her companion left, leaving her alone at the table. My meeting concluded, and as my colleagues rose to leave, I prepared to follow. But as I approached the door, I heard a voice call out in flawless French.

"I love Boston in the summer, don't you?"

The words stopped me in my tracks. My blood ran cold. I slowly turned around to look at the woman.

"Join me?" she said with a smile, gesturing to the empty chair across from her.

I hesitated, debating whether to ignore her and leave or confront the situation head-on. My instincts told me the latter was safer; running might arouse more suspicion. With my heart pounding, I sat down tentatively.

"*Quelle chance,*" she said, her tone light and friendly.

"I'm not sure what you mean," I replied, feigning confusion.

"What are the chances that I would meet you here in France?" she said, her smile growing.

"I think you must be mistaking me for someone else, mademoiselle," I said firmly. "I am sure I do not know you."

"Oh, but I never forget a face. Your French is impeccable, by the way. *Très bon!*"

I gripped my handbag tightly and made to rise from my seat. This woman was dangerous, whether she realized it or not.

"Don't leave so soon, Lady Gold."

I could feel the blood drain from my face. I quickly glanced around the room. There were only two other patrons, both French, and neither seemed to be paying us any attention.

"I am Mademoiselle Antoinette LaFleur," I said, my voice low but firm, "I do not know who this Lady Gold is."

She leaned in slightly, lowering her voice. "Your hair is a little different, of course, but there's no mistaking the beautiful red color. I never forget a face. You would make a stunning model for one of my creations." She extended a gloved hand. "Coco Chanel."

My heart skipped a beat. "The dress designer?" I had read about her in the newspapers.

"Indeed," she said with a playful smile. "But you, madame! Your wedding to Lord Gold was no small affair. It was all over the society pages. Your dress, I must say, was *magnifique!*"

I was thunderstruck. What terrible luck!

She went on, oblivious to my internal panic. "I was in Boston in the summer of 1913. A wonderful city. Everyone was abuzz about your nuptials. I even saw you and your new husband at the theater not long after. You were hard to miss."

She leaned in closer, her voice dropping to a whisper. "Oh yes, I know who you are."

"Mademoiselle, I—"

She placed a hand on mine, her expression softening. "I can only guess what you're doing here. These are dangerous days, are they not?" Her eyes darted around the room before settling back on mine. "I myself am involved in... certain things that are not safe to discuss."

I leaned forward, my voice a harsh whisper. "Please, Mademoiselle Chanel. I cannot stress this enough. Lives—French lives—depend on my identity remaining a secret. If you speak of this to anyone, people will die."

She studied me for a long moment, her expression unreadable. Finally, she said, "Well, whatever it is you're doing, I assume the Boche would not approve."

I nodded slowly, the weight of her words sinking in.

"Then you have nothing to fear from me," she said. "No one will hear a word from my lips." She pressed a finger to her red-painted lips, then smiled. "Now, tell me more about your wedding dress."

Though I was in no mood to discuss fashion, I forced myself to engage, steering the conversation to safe topics—lace, necklines, floral detailing. All the while, a single thought nagged at me: How much weight had I just placed on the promise of a woman I barely knew?

What if, on some cold winter night, too much wine loosened her lips? What then?

For now, I could only hope she was as trustworthy as she claimed. Coco Chanel may have been a genius in fashion, but in this moment, I could only pray that she was also a woman of her word.

Chapter Forty-Two

A LETTER FROM DANIEL

December 31, 1915

TODAY IS a day I will keep forever in my heart because, wonder of wonders, I've received a letter from Daniel! What a fantastic way to make up for the dreary, rainy Christmas day which passed with little more than a lonely glass of wine in my room, and no word from my beloved.

It came this morning just as I was preparing to go out into our village to buy food supplies, dressed as Antoinette LaFleur, of course. I'm so glad I made a deal with Captain Smithwick to have all letters addressed to our Boston apartment intercepted and forwarded to me here, discreetly.

With butterflies in my stomach, I opened the envelope, and a photograph slipped out, landing softly on the floor. Tears welled up as I bent to retrieve it. There he was—my Daniel, leaning against a military vehicle, one hand resting on his hip and a familiar, rakish grin brightening his face. Though a little gaunt, he looked every bit the dashing soldier in his crisp army uniform.

Oh, mercy. How I miss him.

The letter itself brought both joy and sorrow, and I've already read it twice through, committing every word to memory. Here is its content:

December 25, 1915

My dearest Georgia,

Merry Christmas! I hope this letter finds you well. I'm sorry I couldn't write sooner, but the mail service hasn't been very reliable. How is everything in Boston? I hope your father, stepmother, and sister are healthy and thriving.

The conditions here in winter are challenging, to say the least, but my heart is strengthened knowing you are safe, warm, and far away from all this nasty mess of a war.

How do you like the photograph? It was taken in September by a newspaper correspondent who snapped a picture of every soldier in our regiment while we were on a brief reprieve from fighting. We just received our copies, and I'm sending it to you immediately. It's not much of a gift, but it's all I have to offer this year. If all goes well, this conflict will soon be over, and next year, we'll celebrate Christmas together in style. I'll buy you whatever your heart desires!

I must share a peculiar story. On Christmas Eve morning, we were engaged in heavy fighting with the Germans just outside Laventie. By the afternoon, the rain had stopped, and oddly, so had the gunfire from both sides. We began to wonder if the Germans had retreated, though it seemed unlikely given the terrain.

That evening, flasks of rum made their rounds, warming

both body and spirit. A few of us started singing 'Silent Night,' our voices carrying over the stillness of no man's land. Then, to our astonishment, the Germans began to sing back, their voices blending with ours. 'Stille Nacht,' they sang.

As the final verse faded into the cold night air, a cheer rose from the German trenches. Soon after, a voice called out in heavily accented English, "Merry Christmas! We don't shoot at you!"

Now, we had been strictly forbidden by our commanding officers to engage in any kind of Christmas Truce such as the type that had happened last year at various points on the front. After all, how can we expect to win the war when we refuse to shoot at the enemy? Who can explain it? Maybe it's the fact that we have been away from our loved ones too long, or that we harbor the hope that the war is soon coming to an end, but when we saw the Germans clustered around a burning brazier some of us popped our heads up to take a look.

Against orders, a few of us climbed out of the trenches to meet them in no man's land.

For a brief, surreal hour, we exchanged gifts—cigarettes, buttons, hats, and tins of food. I even shared a flask of rum with a fellow named Adalbert, who spoke surprisingly good English. He showed me a photo of his wife, and I, in turn, showed him the picture of you that I carry with me always. He confided that many of his comrades are as weary of the war as we are and unconvinced of its need. I told him that it seems all of us long for it to end.

I can't begin to describe the mix of emotions I felt. Here I was, sharing a flask of rum with someone who, just that morning, had been trying to kill me—and I him. Those who do the most fighting in war are often the ones who wish for it the least.

The impromptu truce ended abruptly when an officer came

*by and barked us back to our trenches. By dawn, the fighting
had resumed, and I haven't seen Adalbert since.*

*Georgia, my love, I'm so very tired of this war. I hope it
ends soon. I miss you terribly.*

Yours,
  Daniel

The letter is now safely tucked away in my bag, though I've
kept the photograph close, propped against a small candle-
holder on my desk.

After reading his words, I felt a bittersweet ache settle in
my chest. How brave he is to cling to hope in such dire circumstances. And how deeply I long to be by his side. Yet, I know
that my own work here in France is just as vital. His letter
reminds me of why I stay, of the importance of every small
action we take against the Boche.

As I write this entry, the rain taps gently on the window,
and I can almost imagine Daniel's voice as I read his words over
again in my mind. His description of the Christmas truce was
both uplifting and haunting. For all the atrocities of war, it's a
testament to the human spirit that even in the darkest times,
there are moments of connection and shared humanity.

Tonight, I'll pray not only for Daniel but also for Adalbert
and his wife. The thought of that German soldier, standing in
no man's land and sharing a photo of his beloved, moves me to
tears. What if Daniel had been born on the other side of the
Channel? Would he, too, be forced to fight for a cause he
doesn't really believe in, longing for a wife he might never see
again? At least Daniel believes very strongly in what he's
fighting for, as do I.

Despite the horrors of this war, moments like the one
Daniel described give me hope for humanity—that perhaps

one day, we might learn to live in peace. I cling to that hope as fervently as I cling to the image of Daniel's face in that photograph.

For now, I'll keep dreaming of the day Daniel and I are reunited, safe and happy in Boston, far away from the mud, the blood, and the chaos of war. Until then, I will hold his words close, a beacon of light in the darkness.

Chapter Forty-Three

BOMBS IN VERDUN!

February 27, 1916

THE BOMBARDMENT STARTED on the morning of the 21st at precisely 7:12 a.m., with a shell landing on the cathedral in Verdun.

The whole hotel building, where I stayed in a room on the second floor, shook mightily, causing my window to shatter inwardly, spraying glass all over.

I shrieked loudly as I dove under my bed covers. The next salvo came only moments later, landing on the main train station. Since then, it has been an almost constant bombardment of the city, with fire crews hopelessly overwhelmed and the town's inhabitants scrambling for any form of protection from the massive German guns, which I'm told are about twenty miles away.

It's very hard to describe the awful, teeth-rattling sound of those guns. It's as if gigantic marching drums were being played by some ancient, angry war god gleefully pounding out his hellish cadence.

Sleep is impossible. Fatigue and panic make for truly terrible companions.

This morning, I was asked by the director of a nearby orphanage to transport eight children and their caretakers out of the city and south to Chaumont-sur-Aire.

At first, I was unsure of the reason why I, in particular, was asked to do this, but then I was told that word had spread of my rather daring nighttime drive to take CV to safety a few months ago.

We set out in a motorized lorry at dawn during a short break in the shelling. Though, as we neared the city limits, a few shells dropped uncomfortably close, landing on the spot where we had just passed. At one point, the lorry swayed violently to the right from the force of a shell blast landing on a nearby factory. Screams from the children were almost as deafening as the explosion, as bricks and splintered wood flew through the air just behind the lorry, covering the street in rubble. Thank God I had a good grip on the steering wheel. If the shell had dropped one second sooner, we would have been buried. I prayed no one was inside that building.

"*Quelle horreur!*" Madame Drouet, one of the chaperones, yelled with her hands covering her ears. She had the misfortune of sitting up front with me as we careened through the streets of Verdun.

"We'll make it!" I yelled back at her in French. The lorry hit a snowy section, causing the end to fishtail. "Hang on, children!" I glanced in my rearview mirror to see the children, most of them crying and hanging on to each other in terror.

Then, just as we'd passed through the town's southern gate, the engine suddenly died. My passengers went silent with fear as I coasted the truck to a stop. The pounding sound of the shelling continued as I jumped out of the vehicle and popped the hood.

I pushed aside my growing panic and firmly gripped the engine crank, gathering my strength to turn it. The engine caught once, ran roughly for a few seconds, and then died again. I knew we had plenty of fuel for the journey, so that wasn't the problem. I tried again, but it was no use.

I quickly opened the driver's side engine cowl to look inside. I had a hunch that whatever it was, it was likely related to the big blast we had just received on the left side of the vehicle from the German shell. The mechanic in charge of this vehicle had told me that he had examined the engine just the night before and deemed it to be in perfect working order; therefore, it was reasonable to suspect that something had happened just a few moments ago. I was taught basic auto repair back in the early days of my training, so I prayed it would be something obvious and not too serious.

Madame Drouet jumped out of the vehicle and rushed over to me. "*Vous ne voulez pas dire que vous êtes mécanicien?*" She was amazed that I would even know anything about engines.

The first thing we were taught about motors is that the electrical components are often the first to fail. In fact, some of the rubber coating on the wiring can be chewed off by small animals mistaking it for food when they huddle into the engine compartments for warmth. This leaves bare wire open and exposed to corrosion, especially in the winter.

I didn't see any signs of that, but after frantically searching the engine for signs of something amiss, I found a dangling cable that seemed out of place. I recognized it as an electrical lead for one of the sparking plugs. The clip had slipped off the tip. I hurriedly re-attached it and, lacking any tools, tightened it as best I could by hand as Madame Drouet looked on in amazement.

I quickly closed the cowl and turned the engine crank handle, motioning for Madame Drouet to get back in the front seat. The engine caught immediately, and the children, capable of so much resilience, cheered. Just as I settled back in behind the wheel and shifted into first gear, another shell hit about seventy feet away. Fortunately, it didn't hit any structures, but we were suddenly showered with snow and mud as I urged the lorry forward.

Finally, we made it to an old dirt road in a little-known route through the forest, the sound of the shelling fading behind us. After about half an hour of slowly making our way through the dense woods, we came to an open field. I pulled the lorry off the road and left the engine running.

"J'ai juste besoin de m'arrêter un instant," I said to the children. "I just need to stop for a moment." Most of them had stopped crying and were staring at me with wide eyes, not saying a word.

I loosened the grip I had on the steering wheel, realizing that I had been squeezing it with all my strength. My hands were shaking. My mouth was dry. I took a gulp of water from my canteen, and for a brief moment, I thought I might be ill, but I swallowed hard and put the vehicle back in gear. The rest of the journey took two hours. I had to stop only once more to re-attach the sparking plug wire. We reached the village of Chaumont-sur-Aire by mid-afternoon, and I delivered the children to a convent there.

I will stay with them overnight and then try to contact my superiors for further orders. I doubt very much they will send me back to Verdun. There's no telling how long the Germans will keep up their attack on the city.

Chapter Forty-Four

THE CLEARING STATION

March 18, 1916

A CASUALTY CLEARING station is usually the first non-mobile medical facility a badly wounded or sick soldier enters after he has fallen. It is a place of grim realities, where hope and despair intermingle, and where lives are saved—or lost—within the span of a heartbeat. I visited for one morning, and the things I saw there will haunt me for the rest of my days.

The sweet, sickly smell of gangrene hung heavy in the air in certain parts of the station, a rancid odor that made my stomach churn. I will never forget it. It clings to the back of the throat, refusing to be swallowed away. While there, I witnessed a soldier lose his leg to the surgeon's saw. His screams, muffled by a leather strap, echoed in the back of my mind long after I left. Another man, pale and skeletal, lay on the operating table with a shrapnel wound to his chest. I watched helplessly as the doctor and nurses worked furiously to stem the bleeding, but their efforts were in vain. His body gave out, and I could feel the weight of collective defeat settle over the room.

Most soldiers, once stabilized, are sent to a convalescence camp where their fate is decided—either a return to duty or a journey elsewhere. But some men don't leave the clearing station alive. Today, I was asked to sit by the bedside of one such soldier, an eighteen-year-old Frenchman named Felix Béchard, who was not expected to recover from his wounds.

He lay propped up on the thin hospital cot, his head wrapped in layers of bandages with only his nose, mouth, and one eye visible. The sight of him took my breath away. How could someone so young have endured so much? Despite his condition, Felix was lucid. His single exposed eye glimmered with a fragile light that seemed almost otherworldly, and his voice, though raspy and frail, carried a surprising clarity.

"What is your name?" I asked in French as I lowered myself onto a small wooden stool by his bedside.

"Felix," he said softly. "Felix Béchard, mademoiselle."

"My name is Antoinette LaFleur," I replied.

He managed a weak smile. "Pleased to meet you, Mademoiselle LaFleur."

"Are you in much pain, Monsieur Béchard?"

"Non, mademoiselle. The nurses have given me something. I feel peaceful."

"That's good," I said, relieved.

"You have an interesting accent. I think you did not grow up in France."

His observation startled me. I had worked tirelessly to perfect my French accent, and no one—not even the Germans —had remarked on it before. Felix, drugged and gravely wounded, had noticed what others had missed. His perceptiveness unnerved me, but I quickly recovered.

"I moved around a great deal as a child," I said, skirting the truth. "Tell me about your family, Monsieur Béchard. Where are they?"

He was silent for a moment. "Gone," he whispered. "My parents died in Maubeuge. My sister too."

My heart ached. I gently placed my hand on his arm, careful not to disturb the bandages. "I am so sorry."

"Thank you," he murmured. "I will be joining them soon, in any case. The doctor has been honest with me."

I hesitated, unsure how to respond. This was my first time speaking to someone who knew he was dying, and I inwardly chastised myself for not knowing what to say.

"Maubeuge," I said finally. "That was at the very beginning, wasn't it?"

"Yes, at the border of Belgium. It was the first French town the Boche attacked. I grew up there."

"Is it a nice place?"

"Very nice," he said, his voice softening. "Or at least it was."

"I will look for it on a map," I promised. "Perhaps someday I will visit."

"I have a sweetheart there," he said suddenly.

"Oh? What is her name?"

"Éloise," he said. "She is the baker's daughter." He motioned weakly to the nightstand beside him. I retrieved a small white envelope, and he bid me to open it. Inside was a photograph of a teenage girl with dark hair and bright, cheerful eyes.

"She's very pretty," I said, studying the picture.

"We have known each other since we were four years old," Felix said. "I asked her to marry me when I was only eight." A faint smile tugged at his lips.

"And did she say yes?" I asked, intrigued.

"*Non,*" he replied with a small chuckle. "She said we were too young. I had to go home and ask my mother if that was true. My mother confirmed it, and I was heartbroken for nearly a whole day."

I couldn't help but smile. "A wise mother."

"Yes," he said. "She made Canelés custard that evening to cheer me up. It helped a little. She also told me to ask Éloise again after I started shaving. She said if it was true love, it would wait."

"And did it?"

"For years, I stared into the mirror, hoping for something to grow on my lip," he said with a wistful laugh. "Éloise and I stayed close friends all the while. Just before the war, I finally asked her again. This time, she said yes."

"How wonderful," I said, though my heart ached knowing their story would have no happy ending.

"We didn't have time for a wedding," he continued, his voice faltering. "When the Boche came to Maubeuge, they killed my family. I rushed to enlist, even though I was too young. Éloise said she would wait for me."

His eye glistened, and I felt tears brimming in my own.

"I already sent her a letter," he said. "But if you do make it to Maubeuge someday, could you do me a favor?"

"Of course," I said, leaning closer. "Anything."

"Find her," he said. "Éloise Lavigne. She is the daughter of Pierre Lavigne, the baker. Tell her that I loved her until the end. Tell her she held my heart prisoner from the time we were children, chasing each other through the summer orchards. Tell her not to be too sad. Her Felix will carry her memory to heaven and cherish it even among the angels, until we meet again."

I promised him I would.

When I left the clearing station, I sat on a bench outside and let the tears come. The cold winter air bit at my cheeks as I wept, my breath visible in short, uneven bursts. I suspect I was not the first person to sit on that bench and cry.

How do these nurses do this day in and day out?

Chapter Forty-Five

CODE

April 27, 1916

YESTERDAY, I was summoned to another farm on the outskirts of a village just inside the Belgian border near Passchendaele. Members of the local intelligence had managed to steal a German wireless set, but their struggle with its operation left them flustered. Since I had experience operating a wireless and a basic knowledge of Morse code, I was asked to assist. I've done many dangerous things during this war, but this task was fraught with uncertainty. It's one thing to smuggle messages or play the role of a harmless French girl. It's quite another to interpret the enemy's very own secrets.

The farm was a modest, weatherworn structure that looked like it had stood for centuries. Like everything else in this region, its stone walls bore silent witness to the upheaval of war. When I arrived, I followed the prearranged knocking rhythm on the wooden door, hoping the signal hadn't been compromised. A gruff, older man in a cap and farmer's overalls opened it cautiously, his keen eyes searching the road behind me before he ushered me in.

"Mademoiselle LaFleur, do come in," he said, closing the door behind us with a firm shove. "I'm Martin." He motioned toward a young man sitting at the kitchen table, looking every bit the academic with his thick wire-rimmed spectacles and carefully combed blond hair. "That's Theo." Then, turning to a serious brunette leaning against the hearth, arms crossed, he added, "Yvonne."

It took me a moment to recognize her. Her hair was cut shorter than when I had met her almost a year ago, when I'd first arrived in France. It was Marianne Chevalier, the switchboard operator who worked beside me for a few weeks. Obviously, she'd also been recruited by Smithwick for a role that I could only guess at.

She must have recognized me, of course, but she gave no indication of it, and neither did I.

Instead, I nodded politely. "Please, call me Antoinette," I said, offering a thin smile. First names give a sense of trust in situations like this, and we needed that.

All three stared at me expectantly, their nervous gazes shifting to the wireless device on the table. It was crude-looking, its wooden carrying case marred by dirt and scratches, yet its significance loomed larger than its shabby exterior.

"Please," Theo said as he vacated his seat, wringing his hands. "You can help? None of us have ever seen anything like this before, and I haven't the foggiest idea how to adjust it. I managed to turn it on, but..."

"Apparently, one of our operatives in Ypres stole this from a house the Germans had occupied and brought it here," Yvonne interjected, her voice steady but taut with the strain of their predicament.

I bent over the wireless, running my fingers over its

controls, noting the German markings and layout. The design was unfamiliar but functional, not unlike the equipment I'd trained on back in England. After making a few adjustments, I heard the faint tapping of Morse signals begin to emerge.

"I'm hearing something," I said. "Quickly—something to write on."

Martin disappeared and returned moments later with a battered notepad and a pencil. As the signals repeated, I started jotting down the series of dots and dashes.

"*Est-ce que quelqu'un parle?*" Martin asked, craning his neck anxiously. "Is it in German?"

"Silence, *s'il vous plaît,*" I murmured, raising my hand to quiet him. My pencil scratched furiously, translating the Morse into letters, but the message made no sense. After three lines, it was clear—the signal was encrypted.

"This is Morse telegraphy," I explained, "but unfortunately, it's encoded. Without the cipher key, it's impossible to know exactly what it says."

"Wait!" Theo said, his voice suddenly hopeful. "Wasn't there a German codebook discovered a few days ago?"

"What codebook?" I asked. My pulse quickened at the thought. If true, it could change everything.

"*Oui, oui,*" Martin added, his face alight with excitement. "Resistance members found it. It's in a nearby village."

"How far?"

"Ten minutes by motorcar," Theo replied.

We wasted no time. Leaving Martin to guard the wireless, we climbed into the battered Renault. Theo, for some reason, decided to drive like a man possessed, his knuckles white on the steering wheel as we raced along the muddy, rutted roads. Trees blurred past, and every distant sound—every far-off gunshot— kept my nerves on edge.

Arriving in the small village, we hurried into a tiny, nondescript restaurant. Yvonne whispered to the owner, a stout man with a bushy mustache, who led us to the back room, locking the door behind us. There, on his desk, lay a small, unmarked notebook.

"The Germans came looking for it," the man said, his voice low and proud. "It fell from an officer's coat pocket two nights ago. I told them I'd seen nothing."

"I almost feel sorry for that officer and what his superiors will do to him," I said as I grabbed the notebook and flipped it open. The pages were filled with dense columns of letters, patterns, and markings—all in German. I worked quickly, cross-referencing my earlier notes against the cipher. Bit by bit, the letters fell into place until the message emerged like a ghost from the fog:

"Kommandant Kemmel to receive first shipment of phosgene shells on the evening of June 14 at St. Eloi. Shells to be fired at dawn the next morning."

The room fell silent.

"What is phosgene?" the café owner asked, his brow furrowed.

"Poison gas," I said grimly. The word left a sour taste in my mouth.

Theo paled. "*Mon Dieu...*"

I swallowed the lump in my throat. "How far to the front?"

"An hour by motorcar," Theo said. "I'll take you."

We sped off again, this time toward the French front line, the air thick with urgency. I kept glancing at the message, willing it not to be true. The thought of men choking, writhing, gasping for breath because of a silent, invisible killer... I forced it from my mind. There was no time for despair.

At the front, a weary French commander met us. His gaunt face and hollow eyes spoke of too many battles fought, and too many lives lost. I handed him the decoded message, and he read it twice before looking up, his expression grave but resolute.

"This will save hundreds of lives," he said, handing the message to his radio operator. "We will alert the troops at St. Eloi immediately. They will be ready."

He gripped my shoulder. "I cannot thank you enough. We knew the Boche would use gas, but we didn't know where or when. You may have just changed the course of this battle."

Theo and I watched as the commander strode off, shouting orders to his men. The weight of what we had done hung heavily in the air.

"Hundreds of lives," Theo whispered, almost to himself.

"Yes," I replied softly, feeling the weight lift—if only slightly. "But the war isn't over yet."

We drove back in silence, the enormity of the day sinking in. I couldn't stop thinking about the gas and the men at St. Eloi. Someone else might be trying to save their soldiers somewhere on the other side of this war.

By the time we reached the village, night had fallen, and the stars gleamed coldly overhead. I tried to look for Yvonne again but was told that she had left the village for another assignment.

I climbed the creaking stairs to my room, too tired to eat, too numb to think. But for now, I could sleep, knowing that we had made a difference—at least today.

Chapter Forty-Six

A BABY

May 18, 1916

JUST WHEN I thought I had seen and done everything imaginable as a secret operative, life surprised me again.

Yesterday, I visited a small farm on the outskirts of a village just on the German side of the front. The family there—two exhausted parents and a quiet boy named Gaston—had been helping to distribute food to French soldiers. Their bravery was remarkable, considering that such actions are strictly forbidden. Most of the food grown on occupied French farms is seized by the Boche for their own use, leaving little for the starving populace.

The family's expressions were gaunt and weary, but I suspected their burdens were heavier than mere hardship. When we concluded our meeting, I thanked them for their courage and prepared to leave, receiving assurances that Gaston would crank the motorcar to life.

As I settled into the driver's seat, Gaston, his dark eyes wide and solemn beneath a tattered gray cap, leaned close and whispered, "Mademoiselle, I need help."

Instantly, my nerves prickled to attention. I scanned the area for immediate danger. "What is it, Gaston?"

"There is an old barn down the road, just before the hairpin turn. Meet me there. Please?"

I hesitated. Any rendezvous under such circumstances carried a risk, but the urgency in his voice left me little choice. "Of course," I said softly. Gaston cranked the engine with surprising strength, and as it roared to life, he gave me one last, searching look before stepping back.

The drive to the barn took only a few minutes, the dirt road uneven beneath my tires. I parked behind a large, bushy hedge, hoping the vehicle was well hidden. Silence fell, broken only by the faint ticking of the engine cooling down.

Soon enough, Gaston appeared, jogging down the path with his thin arms pumping. "Please, come with me," he urged, gesturing for me to follow.

He led me through a side door and up a creaky wooden ladder into the loft of a sagging outbuilding. Sunlight streamed in through gaps in the roof, illuminating motes of dust that floated like ghostly specks above piles of hay and discarded tools. In one dim corner, atop a makeshift mattress of coarse blankets and straw, lay a young girl, curled up on her side and trembling. Her face was damp with sweat, her wide, tearful eyes fixed on me in terror.

"This is my sister, Brigitte," Gaston said in a hushed, serious voice. He hesitated before adding, "My parents are... very hard people. If they find out about this baby, they might kill it."

The words hit me like a physical blow. I could not conceal my shock, and for a moment, I could only stare at the fragile girl who looked far too young to endure such an ordeal.

Gaston pressed on, his voice desperate. "The father is German."

Ah.

I knelt beside her, inhaling deeply to steady myself, and gently took Brigitte's cold, trembling hand in mine. "Hello, Brigitte. I'm Antoinette. We'll do this together, all right?" My voice was calm, though my pulse roared in my ears.

Brigitte's lips quivered, and she whispered, "I loved him."

I swallowed hard as I smoothed damp hair back from her forehead. "I'm sure you did."

"He's been ordered away," she added, her voice breaking. "If he knew about the baby, he would have stayed."

I nodded gently, though her words fell like stones in my chest. If he had been ordered away, there would have been nothing he could've done about it, no matter how he felt. But I couldn't say that to her. Not now.

"Gaston," I said, turning to the boy who hovered anxiously nearby. "I need clean towels and a basin of hot water. I know they will be hard to find but get whatever you can. Quickly!"

While he darted off to find what he could, I busied myself inspecting Brigitte. My heart lurched when I realized how far along she was. There was no time to fetch a doctor. No time for anything but prayer and action.

"Take deep breaths," I instructed, forcing my own voice to remain steady. "In and out. Slowly."

Brigitte gripped my arm with surprising strength. "Will I die?"

"No, *chérie*, you will not. We'll get through this together."

I hoped I sounded more confident than I felt. Women had been having babies since time began, I reasoned. The body knew what to do. But another voice, darker and unwelcome, whispered, Women also die in childbirth every day.

When Gaston returned with a bucket of water and a few

clean towels, I used a torn strip of my cotton slip to mop Brigitte's brow. "You're doing so well," I murmured softly, brushing her hair back again.

As the hours stretched on, her face twisted with pain, her screams muffled by the walls of the old barn. Between contractions, she clung to hope. "Can you find him? Hubert? Tell him about his child?"

I held her hand tightly. "Let's get through today first, Brigitte. One thing at a time."

My mind raced back to an old friend from school who'd trained as a midwife. She had once shared an animated explanation of childbirth, recounting every detail with scholarly enthusiasm. At the time, we were shocked—we were sheltered young women who had never heard of such intimate events before—but now, those words gratefully returned to me, like echoes from another life.

"When you feel the pains, pant like a dog," I instructed. "Blow gently, in and out. It will help you focus."

"Like this?" she asked, breath hitching.

"Yes, that's perfect. You're doing wonderfully."

Finally, the baby crowned, and I coached Brigitte through the final pushes. With a last agonized cry, the child entered the world, red and wailing. With a gush of blood, the afterbirth emerged. I heated my knife over the flame of a candle I had found in a corner and severed the cord, tying it off with a thread I drew from my slip.

Relief flooded through me as I quickly swaddled the newborn in one of Gaston's towels and used the remaining fabric from my slip to clean Brigitte as best I could.

"It's a boy," I announced softly, cradling the baby in my arms.

Brigitte's body sagged with exhaustion, her face pale but peaceful. Yet her next words startled me. "You must take him."

"What?" I stammered.

"You must take him to the village church. The nuns will know what to do." Her voice was barely above a whisper, hollow with resignation. "My parents will never accept him, and I... I can't take care of him alone."

"And you?" I asked gently. "What will you do?"

"I'll wash at the well and make up a story about getting lost in the woods. My mother will be too relieved to ask many questions."

The baby stirred in my arms, its small face scrunching as it whimpered. I stared down at the tiny bundle, feeling a mixture of awe and heartache.

Gaston helped me restart the motorcar, and I drove directly to the village church with the baby safely secured in a basket on the passenger side floor. He didn't so much as whimper once. When the wooden door creaked open, a kind-eyed nun in a black habit took the baby without question, her soft voice murmuring words of comfort I could not hear.

Every muscle in my body ached with exhaustion when I returned to my rented room. I barely managed to pull off my bloodied outer clothing, then fell onto the bed, my mind swirling with images of Brigitte, Gaston, and the fragile life I had carried into safety.

The war has shown me many things, but today will remain etched into my memory forever.

Chapter Forty-Seven

A DANCE, AND NEWS OF DANIEL

June 14, 1916

IT's strange how the human spirit clings so desperately to moments of lightness, even amidst war's darkness. I am now in a village not far from where I delivered the baby. Just inside German-occupied territory.

A private party was held tonight in the village of St. Quentin to which I'd received an invitation—a birthday celebration for Madame Cousineau, the widow of the village's former mayor. The poor man had been killed in battle last year, leaving Madame Cousineau a much-admired figure, respected for her stoic endurance and quiet generosity.

She had hired the public house for the evening, and though wartime austerity had made luxuries like fine wine and pastries a rarity, somehow, there were just enough to make the evening merry. The candles flickered in their sconces, casting a soft, golden light on the room, and the steady hum of conversation and laughter intertwined with the mournful strains of an accordion. For a few hours, the war beyond the village square seemed to fade. Except for the fact that several German officers were there—one could not host such a party without their presence—one could almost pretend the war was over.

I sat beside Madame Cousineau at a corner table, exchanging pleasantries as we nibbled on slices of gâteau and sipped wine. We spoke of small things—how the rains had finally stopped, how the baker had found a way to stretch flour supplies for another week. It was, I suppose, the sort of banal chatter that people use to ward off the reality of life in occupied France. The evening was going well when something odd happened.

At one point, I excused myself to use the powder room. Directed to the second floor, I followed a quiet corridor and found it at the end of the hallway. As I approached, a small window overlooking the courtyard caught my attention. The window was partially open, and faint voices speaking in German drifted in from below.

Curious, I leaned closer to peer outside. To my astonishment, I spotted a woman who looked strikingly familiar—Marianne Chevalier. She stood just a few feet away from a German officer, her posture composed, her back partially turned toward me.

Though I couldn't make out her words, the cadence and tone of her voice felt unmistakably familiar. Could it really be her? I strained to get a better look, my heart racing. If it was Marianne, what was she doing here—and why was she speaking with a German officer?

I watched as their conversation came to an end. The officer turned sharply and walked back toward the building while the woman—if it truly was Marianne—moved in the opposite direction, disappearing into a small, wooded area at the edge of the courtyard. I remained frozen for a moment, staring after her in puzzlement.

Just as I returned to my seat, Captain Smithwick appeared out of nowhere, his presence slicing through the evening like a blade.

"*Bonsoir, mesdames*," he said, his French impeccable as always.

Madame Cousineau, clearly delighted by his sudden arrival, turned toward him with a warm smile. "*Ah, bonsoir,* Monsieur Favreau!" she exclaimed. "This is my friend, Mademoiselle Antoinette LaFleur. We met only days ago but have already become fast friends. Antoinette, this is Monsieur Berton Favreau. He is quite new to our little town."

I rose to greet him, my face a mask of polite curiosity as I extended my hand. "*Enchanté,* Monsieur Favreau," I said, carefully entering into the charade. "May I inquire what brings you to our quiet village?"

"I am here to help teach at the school," he replied without missing a beat. "They are in need of a mathematics instructor. I have traveled from my hometown of Hautmont to fill the role until a more permanent solution can be found."

"A noble undertaking," Madame Cousineau said, clearly charmed. "I do hope you might stay longer, Monsieur Favreau. The children would benefit greatly from a man of your talents."

She smiled at him—too warmly, I thought—and I wondered if Madame Cousineau, despite her widow's black, might see this "Monsieur Favreau" as a candidate for something more than mathematics instruction. Or perhaps she knew as I did: that his presence here had nothing to do with arithmetic and everything to do with the war. In matters like these, I am rarely told who else is working with British Intelligence or the '*réseau*', lest any interrogation makes me a liability.

Captain Smithwick gave a small, elegant bow, then extended his hand toward me as the accordionist struck up a new tune. "Mademoiselle, might I have this dance?"

I glanced at Madame Cousineau, whose lips twitched—gracefully concealing what I suspected was irritation at being so suddenly overlooked. But what could I do? I couldn't exactly say no to Captain Smithwick, not when I knew that his sudden appearance was no accident.

We moved to the center of the room and began to step to the music, when suddenly I recognized the tune. Out here, in occupied France, the musician played "Road to Mandalay." The music caught me off guard, tugging at a part of me I keep hidden, and I felt a deep ache rise in my chest as thoughts of Daniel flooded in. Was he safe tonight? Was he hearing a tune like this, thinking of me as I thought of him?

We danced silently for a moment until I said in a quiet voice, "I think I just saw Marianne."

"Marianne?"

"She worked with me as a switchboard operator. You know her, Marianne Chevalier."

Smithwick glanced surreptitiously around the room.

"She's gone now. I also encountered her in Belgium only a month ago," I added.

"She was assigned to help the local underground there. I recruited her myself." Smithwick looked puzzled. Are you sure she's here? I did not assign her to this place."

"Not completely sure, no. I saw her from a distance. She was talking to a German officer outside."

"Hmm, I'll have to look into it. She could have gotten new orders, but I haven't learned of them yet. That can happen, though I can't imagine why she would be talking to a German officer on her own." Smithwick leaned in closer for just a moment. "However. I'm here to deliver some news to you. I have word of your husband."

The words struck me like a blow, and I felt the blood drain from my face. My steps faltered. "Is Daniel all right? Where did you see him?"

"He's fine," Smithwick replied quickly, anticipating my fear. "I can't tell you where, of course, but I saw him a week ago in Belgium. He was seated with his unit, sharing a drink on a cold evening. I didn't speak to him, but he was laughing—he seemed well enough. Sound in health and spirits."

Relief washed over me in a dizzying rush, and I had to bite my lip to keep the tears from falling. The war has taught me to expect the worst and steel myself against news I dread hearing. So often, I live in a constant state of anxiety, the unknown gnawing at me like a persistent ache. I wake at night in cold sweats, my mind filled with images I try desperately to chase away. To know that Daniel was alive and laughing—laughing!—just a week ago is like a small miracle, a momentary reprieve from the weight I carry.

"Thank you," I whispered. "You cannot imagine what that means to me."

"How are you faring?" Captain Smithwick asked, his voice softer now. "From all reports, you've done your job with admirable aplomb."

"I'm glad to hear my efforts are appreciated," I replied, trying to keep my voice steady. "It hasn't been easy, I won't lie. But I'm learning to be quite comfortable as Antoinette LaFleur."

Smithwick's gaze drifted toward the room as we danced. "Not everyone has done so well, I'm afraid."

"Oh?" I asked carefully.

"We lost two operatives last week. One was betrayed by an

informant and executed. The other was killed by a faulty grenade during sabotage work."

My stomach dropped, and a chill passed through me. "Oh, mercy."

Captain Smithwick's face remained impassive, but his voice held a weight that could not be masked. "I tell you this only as a reminder of the stakes we face."

"And what are you really doing here tonight?" I asked quietly. As grateful as I was for the news of Daniel, I knew full well that Captain Smithwick wouldn't travel out of his way simply to offer a personal report.

His lips brushed close to my ear as he whispered, "We expect the arrival of a high-value target—Field Marshal Franz Keitel. Should you spot anyone of his rank entering the '*hôtel de ville*', report it immediately. You know what to look for."

"Yes," I said firmly. "Understood."

The song ended, and Captain Smithwick released my hand, giving me a small but satisfied smile before bowing politely. Without another word, he turned and disappeared into the crowd.

I returned to my table and sat down, still reeling from the encounter. I scanned the room, hoping to catch sight of him again—but he was gone, vanished as suddenly as he had appeared. It was as though he had melted into the shadows, leaving behind only the faintest ripple in his wake.

I sipped my wine, my mind racing with thoughts of Daniel, Field Marshal Keitel, and the ever-present peril of the life I now lead. How strange it is to waltz on the knife's edge, to smile and dance when the ground beneath you could give way at any moment.

But for now, I will dance. I will smile. And I will watch.

Chapter Forty-Eight

A DANGEROUS MISSION

August 19, 1916

A YEAR HAS PASSED, and I find that I've almost settled into a kind of strange normalcy. It never ceases to amaze me how adaptable the human spirit really is. Each morning, I assume the role of Mademoiselle Antoinette LaFleur almost as naturally as donning a familiar dress. My real identity fades into the background, submerged under layers of deception and duty. Yet, one thing I'll never grow accustomed to is the immediacy of danger that shadows my every step.

Yesterday, I was invited to a cocktail party by Hauptmann Gottlieb Auerswald, a German officer I encountered at the library in the town where I am presently stationed. It wasn't a chance meeting, of course. My assignment had been to cross paths with him, gain his trust, and secure an invitation to this very event. The party was being held at a grand estate appropriated by the Germans from the town's mayor—a large, elegant home with high ceilings, expensive furnishings, and a distinct sense of unease in every room.

Hauptmann Auerswald himself was not particularly remarkable. A portly man in his early forties with thinning blond hair, a crooked nose, and a predatory gleam in his eyes, he carried himself with an air of inflated importance. His uniform was spotless, and his boots polished to a mirror shine, but his appearance did little to mask the impression of someone who had likely been in one too many bar fights in his youth. Nevertheless, he was my gateway to a far more critical target.

A little fluttering of the eyelashes, and I had my invitation. That was the easy part.

Staying as a guest at the estate was Generalmajor Felix Scholz, a high-ranking officer on his way to the front. It was known through our network that Generalmajor Scholz was carrying orders for a major attack on Allied trenches planned in three days' time. Telephone wires had been cut by French operatives and the Germans were forced to relay messages in person. Generalmajor Scholz not only carried the orders but was going to help plan the attack. My instructions were to sneak into his room and search for the orders. I was given a camera which was cleverly disguised as a pocket watch to take snapshots

"A pleasure to see you again, Mademoiselle LaFleur," Hauptmann Auerswald greeted me at the door, his round face lighting up as he took my arm. I wore my finest summer dress for the occasion—a royal blue frock trimmed with lace at the collar and cuffs, adorned with dainty pearl buttons running down the bodice. My braided hair was concealed under a silk velvet hat—Germans thought red hair was ugly, so I wore hats as a rule—and I carried a matching drawstring purse that concealed my essential tools of the trade.

"You look enchanting," he said, his gaze lingering a little

too long. I forced a demure smile and allowed him to escort me inside.

The estate was abuzz with activity. German officers mingled with enlisted men, their laughter and chatter filling the air. French servants moved briskly between rooms, serving an impressive spread of wine, cheese, and pastries—a rare indulgence in occupied France. The scent of fresh flowers mingled with the acrid undertone of tobacco smoke, creating a dissonance that set my nerves on edge.

After an obligatory round of introductions, during which I endured the leers of several officers, I feigned an interest in the architecture of the house. "It reminds me so much of the home I grew up in," I said, batting my eyelashes just enough to nudge Hauptmann Auerswald into action.

"Allow me to give you a tour," he offered, clearly pleased to play the role of gallant host.

He led me through the grand halls, pointing out various features with pride. When we ascended the sweeping staircase to the upper level, my heart quickened. At the far end of the corridor, Hauptmann Auerswald gestured toward a door. "That is where Generalmajor Scholz is staying," he said casually, though I noted the subtle shift in his tone—a hint of reverence or perhaps fear.

As we returned to the main floor, Hauptmann Auerswald introduced me to a group of officers gathered in a study. One of them, a grizzled veteran with steel-blue eyes, assessed me with an unsettling intensity. "Where have you been hiding this one, Auerswald?" he remarked, his voice as cold as his gaze.

"She is my guest for the evening," the Hauptmann replied, his tone possessive. I suppressed a shudder.

When the opportunity arose, I excused myself under the pretense of freshening up. Navigating the maze of hallways, I found the staircase leading back to the second floor. My pulse raced as I approached the door to Scholz's room. From my purse, I retrieved a lock-picking tool disguised as an innocuous Swiss Army-style knife. The lock yielded quickly to my practiced hands.

Inside, the room was dimly lit, the faint scent of tobacco lingering in the air. My eyes immediately scanned for anything out of place. In the bottom drawer of a mahogany bureau, I found a leather satchel. My hands trembled as I opened it, revealing a large white envelope stamped with official seals. Inside were the orders I'd been sent to find. Using the camera, I carefully photographed each page, the tiny click of the shutter almost deafening in the silence.

Just as I returned the satchel to its original position, I heard footsteps in the corridor. My blood turned to ice. Without thinking, I slipped into a wardrobe and eased the door shut, my heart pounding so loudly I feared it would give me away.

The door to the room creaked open, and heavy boots crossed the floor. I gripped the pistol in my purse, my finger hovering over the trigger. If discovered, I knew my options were grim: capture, torture, and likely execution. The thought of Daniel flashed through my mind, and I sent a silent prayer heavenward.

The intruder lingered for what felt like an eternity, rummaging through drawers before finally departing. When I heard the key turn in the lock, I allowed myself to exhale. My legs felt like jelly as I emerged from the wardrobe and hurried back to the party, careful to compose myself before rejoining Hauptmann Auerswald.

"You were gone a while," he remarked, his tone laced with suspicion.

"I'm afraid I'm not feeling well," I replied, feigning discomfort and making myself blush. "Perhaps it—it was something I ate." My tone seemed to imply that it was actually a woman's issue, and I counted on his embarrassment about such things to not pursue the matter.

I was right, as he immediately dropped the issue and called for a taxicab to take me home. Only once I was safely back in my flat did I allow myself to crumble, the strain leaving me drained and trembling. Tomorrow, I would deliver the film to my contact and complete the mission. For now, I could only hope for a few hours of rest before the next challenge arose.

Chapter Forty-Nine

A SEED OF DOUBT

September 20, 1916

THE WAR HAS a way of weaving unexpected patterns, pulling familiar threads through unfamiliar places. I was stunned when I received my latest assignment and found that I would work alongside Marianne—though she is now calling herself Claire Villeneuve. Captain Smithwick has been unable to confirm one way or another if it really was her I saw at the party in June, which raises more questions than answers.

Now, here she is again, inexplicably reappeared, and assigned to this critical task with me. I've received my orders through a secret written note.

I couldn't help myself. I turned to her as we left the rendezvous point and began walking toward Saint-Loup. "Claire, why were you at Madame Cousineau's party?"

She glanced at me sharply, her expression carefully neutral. "Madame who?"

"Madame Cousineau. She's the widow of the mayor of the

village of St. Quentin. She held a party to which I was invited in June."

"I'm sorry. I just don't know what you are talking about. I was in Paris in June of this year. Of course, I saw you in Belgium. I think that was in April when the German wireless was found."

"Oh," I said, doubt nagging at me. But it was possible I was mistaken. I only saw her from the back, although I could swear I heard her voice. Her explanation of being in Paris was plausible albeit almost impossible to check. We were often kept in the dark about each other's work to protect the network. I pushed the thoughts aside, focusing instead on the task at hand.

The mission was quite common in terms of working with the RRL, though it was no less dangerous. The task involved delivering covert communication; the packet we carried was small yet potentially devastating for the enemy. It contained maps outlining German troop movements, supply routes, and artillery positions—information smuggled at great risk by the local resistance and compiled by British Intelligence. Additionally, it included a coded message directing a key contact within the Allied forces on how to counter the German strategy. Our responsibility was to deliver it to a tailor in the village of Saint-Loup, a known safe house for French underground operatives. The information needed to reach its destination without delay or interception. It was considered better for two women to deliver the note in order to raise less suspicion. These days, it had become increasingly rare for a French woman to be out in public alone.

It took us about an hour to walk along the rutted dirt road to the village where we are currently stationed. Gasoline-powered vehicles in this area have almost all been repurposed by the Germans or taken outright. Walking on foot was deemed less suspicious than horse and cart.

We were dressed as simple farm women; our shawls pulled tightly around our shoulders against the slight chill in the air. Marianne carried a basket of apples, a prop to bolster our cover, while I kept the satchel containing the packet strapped securely around my waist.

"I'm sorry I didn't get a chance to talk to you after we found that wireless in Belgium," I said.

She smiled faintly. "I've been moving around a lot, like you, I imagine. Assignments come quickly, and we don't always have time for reunions."

"That's true. In any case, it's good to see you again. I enjoyed our time together during training."

She didn't respond immediately, and when I glanced at her, she seemed deep in thought.

"Yes, I did too," she said finally. It was as if she had to consider the thought momentarily before committing to the sentiment.

The village of Saint-Loup lay quiet as we approached. A small church steeple rose in the middle of the village, and the faint hum of activity drifted toward us. Farmers tended to their fields, a cart creaked as it rolled down the main street, and a group of children played near a fountain.

But the tranquility was deceptive. As usual, German soldiers patrolled the square, their rifles slung casually over their shoulders, their boots thudding on the cobble stones.

The tailor's shop was tucked away on the edge of the village, its faded sign swaying gently in the breeze. I tugged at the edge of my shawl—the prearranged signal—and we entered. The shopkeeper, a wiry man with sharp eyes, greeted us with a wary nod and led us to a small back room.

I removed the packet from my satchel and handed it to

him. He examined it briefly before opening a drawer beneath the counter and hiding the papers under a sheaf of sewing patterns.

"*Merci,*" he said softly. "This will make a difference."

I nodded, then glanced at Marianne, who stood near the door, her posture tense. "Claire, everything all right?"

"Yes," she said quickly, her tone clipped.

The shopkeeper's gaze flicked between us, his brow furrowed. "You weren't followed, were you?"

"Absolutely not," I said firmly. "We were careful."

The village square seemed quieter than before, though the soldiers still lingered near the town hall.

"We should take the side streets," I murmured, steering Marianne away from the square.

We moved quickly but carefully, the narrow alleyways offering some measure of cover, the cobblestones uneven beneath our feet.

"It's not much further," Marianne said, her voice low.

As we rounded a corner, the sound of boots echoed behind us. My heart leaped into my throat. Marianne grabbed my arm, her grip firm but steady.

"Keep walking," I whispered, my tone calm but urgent.

We quickened our pace, trying to maintain the appearance of two women going about their business. But the footsteps grew louder, closer.

We turned another corner and came face-to-face with two German soldiers. My breath caught, but Marianne didn't hesitate.

"*Halt!*" one of the soldiers barked. "*Was machen Sie hier in diesem Dorf?*"

I was ready to put on a pretense of not being unable to understand him, when Marianne stepped forward, her expression calm. "*Entschuldigung, mein Herr,*" she said in flawless

German, which surprised me. Unlike my German, hers held only a small hint of a French accent. *"Wir bringen Äpfel zu meiner Tante. Sie ist krank und kann sie nicht selbst holen."* She told them we were delivering apples to her aunt who was ill and couldn't fetch them herself.

The soldier eyed us suspiciously but seemed to accept her explanation. He nodded, motioning for us to continue.

"Danke," Marianne said with a slight bow of her head.

We walked on, my pulse racing.

Once we were safely away from the soldiers, I let out a shaky breath. "That was too close."

Marianne nodded, her face unreadable.

"I didn't know you spoke German so well." I said, "Impressive."

My mind went back again to that meeting in the courtyard of Madame Cousineau's party. If it wasn't her that I heard and saw there, it was an uncanny resemblance to whoever it was.

"I worked for a German-speaking employer in the Elsace before the war, translating letters and managing communications. It's one of the reasons I was recruited—my German is passable enough to avoid suspicion."

"I was recruited partially for that reason too. But..."

Marianne cut me off. "Let's just get out of here."

As we made our way back toward the outskirts of the village, I couldn't help but feel that something was out of place. I couldn't shake a lingering unease in my gut, and yet I can't quite identify why I was bothered.

Now that I'm back in my room, I ponder the day's events. I'll end this entry with this thought: Trust is the foundation of everything we do. But in times like these, even trust can feel like a luxury.

Chapter Fifty

MONSTERS

September 26, 1916

I'M BACK from behind enemy lines now, and I've been here for a few days, although the front isn't far away. It's becoming increasingly difficult to cross enemy lines as the war progresses, and it's starting to take its toll. Each time, it usually requires complex planning from local operatives using established escape routes and coded messages. So far, I've been fortunate, as the Germans tend to underestimate women, but I'm beginning to wonder how long I can maintain this before either I or someone who is assisting me gets caught. My pulse races every time I pass a checkpoint. I know it's necessary for me to be able to move across the lines, but I plan to discuss it with Captain Smithwick soon to see if we can reduce how often it happens.

In any case, today offered a rare gift: free time. I rarely find a moment to breathe amidst the chaos, so I arranged to meet Nurse Haley Higgins for lunch. When I learned she'd be stationed in Amiens for a few weeks, coinciding with my own assignment, I couldn't pass up the chance to reconnect.

How fortuitous!

The café I chose, Café de l'Homme, is a gem tucked along one of Amiens' bustling main roads. Known for serving the most divine French onion soup, it provided a rare pocket of comfort. As I sat at a little table beneath the dappled shade of a sycamore tree, the autumn sun casting its golden glow on the cobblestone street, it was almost possible to forget the war raging to the west.

"*Bonjour*, Mademoiselle LaFleur," Nurse Higgins greeted me warmly, her Bostonian accent so strong that it came out sounding like "bonne chure." I fought back the small wave of homesickness this brought on. Even though she was nearly six feet tall, she folded herself into the ornate wrought-iron chair with surprising elegance, her long, capable fingers tucking stray curls of chestnut hair back under her nurse's cap.

"Hello again, Nurse Higgins," I replied with a smile, extending my hand across the small round table. Her firm handshake conveyed the same confidence she'd exuded during our first meeting.

She leaned in slightly, her voice dropping to a conspiratorial whisper. "How are you? Safe, I see?" Though she didn't know the full extent of my work for British Intelligence, her sharp intuition had already surmised that I wasn't just an ordinary Frenchwoman.

"As well as can be expected," I said, keeping my answer deliberately vague. "And you? How are things?"

Her expression darkened, the weight of her experiences clouding her features. "Trying, as always. But we must carry on. The men depend on us more than ever."

I nodded, silently admiring her resilience. "I don't know how you do it," I said sincerely. The horrors I'd witnessed—

mangled limbs, soldiers clinging to life, the ceaseless specter of death—still haunted me, and I was far removed from the medical frontlines.

The waiter brought our simple meal of soup and bread with brisk efficiency. The aroma of caramelized onions, melted cheese, and fresh-baked baguettes filled the air, momentarily lifting the somber mood.

We had just begun eating when the ground beneath us began to tremble.

"What on earth?" Haley exclaimed, setting her coffee cup down as its contents rippled. The delicate china rattled on its saucer, and a low, guttural rumble echoed through the streets.

I froze, my pulse quickening. It wasn't the first time I'd felt the ground quake, but this was different. The tremors grew stronger, rattling the windows of nearby buildings and sending nervous glances skyward.

"Wait," Haley said suddenly, pushing her chair back and standing. "Do you hear that?"

The sound was unmistakable now—a deep, mechanical growl that seemed to come from everywhere at once. My first thought was aircraft, but as I scanned the sky, there was no sign of planes.

"No," I said, shaking my head. "Not propellers. It's something else."

Moments later, the source of the noise came into view. Turning the corner onto the cobbled street was a monstrous steel machine, its lumbering frame clanking and grinding with each movement. Belching thick black smoke from its undercarriage, the vehicle crawled forward on massive metal tracks, its angular frame gleaming dully in the sunlight.

"Oh my goodness," I breathed, gripping the edge of the table as my breath caught in my throat.

Haley gasped beside me. "Mark I tanks!" she exclaimed, her

voice a mix of awe and disbelief. "I heard rumors they'd be deployed, but I never thought I'd see one!"

The tank's turret swiveled slowly as it passed, the machine-gun barrel jutting from its side like the snout of some great metal predator. Behind it, a second tank rumbled into view, followed by a convoy of lorries carrying British infantry.

The spectacle brought the street to a halt. Pedestrians stood frozen, their faces a mixture of fear and fascination. A few scattered children, their eyes wide with curiosity, darted after the convoy, shouting and pointing as they followed the mechanical beasts down the road.

"I heard about these machines," Haley said, her voice hushed. "They can cross trenches, mow down barbed wire, and withstand machine gun fire."

"And terrify everyone in their path," I added, unable to tear my eyes away.

We watched in silence as the convoy passed, the tanks' engines roaring like thunder, shaking the very ground beneath us. Though their presence was a sign of Allied strength, I couldn't help but feel a deep unease. These hulking machines represented a new kind of warfare—cold, impersonal, and relentless.

When the noise finally began to fade, Haley sat back down with a sigh, her expression pensive.

"Do you think they'll make a difference?" I asked, breaking the silence.

"They have to," she replied firmly. "But even if they do, it won't end the war overnight. The Central Empires won't give up so easily."

I nodded, lifting my coffee cup in a small, solemn toast. "To hope," I said softly.

Haley raised her cup, a flicker of determination in her eyes. "To hope."

Chapter Fifty-One

THE RESCUE AND REVELATION

October 15, 1916

I WRITE these words with a somber heart.

This mission was unlike any I had faced before. Its importance was clear from the outset, and I was both honored and terrified to be entrusted with its success. We were to collect an Allied operative known only by his code name: Rook. He was not just any courier—he was the mastermind behind an intricate network that spanned several occupied territories, a web responsible for feeding intelligence to the Allies. If the Germans found him and broke him, it would not only compromise underground operations but also lead to the deaths of countless covert French fighters and Allied agents. Unfortunately, Rook had recently become ill from weeks of malnutrition and hiding and needed medical care and respite. It was crucial that he be smuggled out of occupied France immediately.

With the oncoming dusk, I crossed the line back into occupied territory just after 18:00. It went smoothly again, but my hands shook as I drove away from the checkpoint and again I wondered yet again what kind of toll each crossing was beginning to take on me.

Partially due to the success of our mission last month, I was once again paired with Claire Villeneuve, also known as Marianne Chevalier. The choice of our team was unconventional: two women posing yet again as simple farm women. As before, the logic behind it was sound—women were less likely to draw attention, particularly in occupied villages where German soldiers had grown accustomed to seeing local women carrying out daily chores. We both spoke German, and Marianne had, for a while as a child, lived not far from the village, and knew the area.

Our orders were clear: travel by horse and cart to the village, locate Rook and extract him before he could be moved to a more secure location. The operation relied on a carefully planned relay. Local operatives were stationed at intervals to provide temporary shelter, intelligence updates, or even alternate routes if German patrols were spotted. The plan was fluid enough to adapt to changing circumstances. The first location was two hours away by cart, and our job was to get Rook there using rural backroads and bypassing main thoroughfares patrolled by the Boche. If we were questioned, we would explain that Rook (disguised as a mute uncle) was a shell-shocked war victim needing care at the next village.

The village looked deceptively ordinary as we approached. The narrow streets were lined with stone cottages, the small-paned windows firmly closed against the autumn chill. Smoke curled lazily from a few chimneys, and the faint murmur of voices drifted from a small café. German soldiers patrolled in pairs, their rifles slung casually over their shoulders. Though they seemed relaxed, their very presence was a stark reminder of the danger we faced.

We had left our cart hidden in a wooded grove on the village's edge and continued on foot. I carried an empty satchel meant for Rook's escape tools—a set of false identity papers, money, and a map marked with safe routes.

Our first contact was a quiet young man who called himself Luc, who worked at a blacksmith shop near the outskirts. He confirmed that the way was clear and guided us to Rook's hiding place. When we got to within a hundred meters of the place, he stopped.

"There's an old man named Jacques Chaucier and his twelve-year-old grandson Denis living there. Jacques will take you to him." Luc said and then left without another word.

The safe house was an unassuming stone cottage near the village square. Its faded shutters and peeling plaster made it look abandoned, but a slight movement of one of the window curtains signaled that it was occupied. Marianne and I approached cautiously, keeping to the shadows.

"I'll stay out here and keep watch," she said as I opened the front door.

"But surely, Jacques' grandson could..."

"I think it's better if I do it." Her insistence caught me off guard.

I nodded, though something about her eagerness made me pause. I told myself it was nothing—just nerves, a common companion in our line of work. The door creaked as I stepped inside, where the air was thick with the scent of damp stone and wood smoke.

"Jacques?" I called softly, closing the door behind me.

A boy emerged from the shadows, his face pale and gaunt but his eyes determined. He clutched a battered oil lamp in his hands, the flame flickering dimly in the gloom.

"Jacques passed away last week from pneumonia," the boy said, his voice steady despite his age. "I'm Denis, his grandson."

I stared at him, momentarily stunned. "You've been here alone? Taking care of... him?"

Denis nodded. "I promised Grandpère I would. He said it was important."

My heart clenched. Such bravery in someone so young was both humbling and heartbreaking. "Thank you, Denis. You've done more than anyone could ask. Now, take me to him."

Denis turned and led me through the small, cluttered house to a small room that was obviously a larder, though its shelves now stood bare. He lifted a piece of linoleum and revealed a trapdoor with a simple latch.

"He's down here," Denis said, his voice quieter now, pulling up the trapdoor and handing me the oil lamp.

I descended into the cellar, the air growing colder and mustier with each step. The space was dimly lit by a single candle. In the corner, on a makeshift cot, lay a man whose presence was almost as faint as the flickering flame.

Rook was a shadow of a man, his face hollowed by hunger and illness. His breathing was labored, his skin pale and clammy.

"Rook?" I said softly, kneeling beside him.

His eyes fluttered open, glassy but aware. "You... made it," he rasped.

"Yes, and we're getting you out of here," I assured him, though doubt gnawed at me. Could he even survive the journey?

Denis knelt beside me, his small hands clutching a cup of water, which he offered to Rook. "He's been like this for days," Denis whispered.

I placed a hand on the boy's shoulder. "You've done well. We'll take it from here."

Suddenly, from above, I heard the unmistakable sound of voices—German voices. My blood turned to ice as I strained to hear.

"They're here somewhere," one of them barked.

And then, Marianne's voice.

"There must be a cellar of some kind. The boy and the old man and our target will be with her."

Her words, spoken in perfect German, struck me like a physical blow. Betrayal crashed over me in waves, leaving me momentarily paralyzed. Marianne—my friend, my comrade—was a double agent.

Denis tugged at my sleeve, snapping me back to the moment. "There's a way out," he whispered urgently.

"Show me," I said, my voice barely audible over the pounding in my ears.

Denis scurried to the far wall, where he pushed aside a stack of crates to reveal a narrow tunnel, barely wide enough for a grown adult. "Grandpère and I started digging this last year."

"Where does it lead?" I asked.

"To the barn. There's a car hidden there," Denis said, his words rushed but clear.

I glanced back at Rook, who was barely conscious. "We have to move him."

With Denis's help, I managed to lift Rook onto my back, his frail body alarmingly light. The tunnel was dark and cramped, the air thick with the scent of earth. Denis led the way, holding the oil lamp aloft to guide us.

Behind us, the sound of boots thundered through the house. The Germans had found the trapdoor. My heart raced as I urged Denis to move faster.

The tunnel opened into a small barn, its interior cloaked in shadows. In the corner sat a motorcar, its body covered with a tarp. Denis yanked the tarp off, revealing the vehicle beneath.

"Do you know how to drive?" Denis asked, his voice trembling.

"Yes," I said, though my hands shook as I placed Rook in the back seat as quickly as I could. In a desperate hurry, Denis shoved open the barn doors that creaked on rusty hinges, then scrambled in beside Rook, cradling the man's head with surprising tenderness.

I yanked at the crank handle, praying the car would start. The engine sputtered and coughed, then roared to life; I vaulted into the driver's seat just as the figures of German soldiers appeared at the open barn door, their rifles raised.

I slammed my foot on the accelerator, the car lurching forward with a deafening roar, right toward them. They sprang out of the way, and bullets ricocheted off the metal frame as we drove through the barn's entrance and into the darkening evening.

I knew I couldn't go to the agreed-upon safe house. Marianne would know of its location. I prayed that the occupants of that house would somehow escape as she no doubt would tell the Germans about it or maybe already had. I had to come up with another plan, and fast.

"How much petrol...?" I began.

"It's full," Denis said simply.

I breathed a quick prayer of thanks for that miracle, considering the fuel rations that the Germans had imposed. My mind raced to find an alternative destination. Then it occurred to me: the convent in Chaumont-sur-Aire, where I had delivered the children last February—they would have enough medical supplies there to stabilize Rook and get word to the underground. It was highly likely Marianne would not be aware of its existence. It would take half the night to get there, but it was the only place I could think of.

"Do you know the way to Chaumont-sur-Aire?" I asked Denis.

"I was born there. I lived there until my parents were killed a year ago by the Bosche." He replied, "I know a way there through the forests. There is a spot where we might pass through the line in the darkness with the car. The Germans sometimes don't patrol that part of the forest in the middle of the night. The trees are very dense there, and it's a long way from the nearest village."

Another small miracle.

After leaving the edge of the village, the road was rough and uneven, the tires skidding on muddy patches. Rook groaned in the back seat, his condition worsening with every jolt and turn. Denis whispered words of encouragement to him, his voice amazingly steady despite the chaos.

I drove with a singular focus, navigating the dark, winding roads with only the faint moonlight and Deni's instructions to guide me. The forest closed around us, the trees forming a shadowy tunnel stretching endlessly. At some points, we were not even driving on any kind of road or even a trail and at one point, the car's wheels sank into a patch of mud. I cursed under my breath as I tried to free the vehicle, the engine whining in protest. Denis jumped out to push, his small frame straining against the car's weight. If we couldn't free it, this mission and possibly our lives would be lost. With a final heave, we broke free, the tires spinning wildly as we lurched forward.

"We've done it. We're across the line." Said Denis about 10 minutes later as the car climbed onto a small road half over-grown with vegetation that offered at least some solid footing.

I breathed a long sigh and could feel tears welling up in relief.

Meanwhile, the Rook's breathing grew shallower, each gasp a painful reminder of how close we were to losing him.

An hour later, the convent suddenly loomed ahead, its stone walls bathed in the faint glow of moonlight filtering through the heavy clouds. The iron gates creaked softly as I pushed them open, their weight more psychological than physical as they seemed to hold back the world outside. A lone lantern flickered near the entrance, casting long shadows across the cobblestone courtyard. The faint scent of lavender and damp earth filled the cool night air, starkly contrasting the chaos we'd just escaped.

I pulled the car to a stop, its sputtering engine finally giving out. Denis scrambled out first, his face pale but determined as he ran to the large wooden door and banged the brass knocker. The sound echoed hollowly before being swallowed by the thick silence of the night. For a moment, I feared no one would answer, but then a soft glow appeared behind the stained glass panels of the door.

It creaked open, revealing Sister Beatrice, her kind face lined with age but her sharp eyes taking in the scene with practiced efficiency. In spite of the hour, she was fully dressed, her wimple white against her black habit and veil, her hands clasped tightly around a lantern. Behind her, two younger sisters hovered, their expressions a mixture of concern and curiosity.

"Soeur Beatrice," I said quickly, my voice trembling with urgency. "We need sanctuary. Please."

Her gaze moved to Denis, then to the back seat of the car where Rook lay slumped, his chest barely rising. Without hesitation, she stepped aside and motioned us in. "Bring him quickly. We'll do what we can."

The sisters sprang into action. One of the younger nuns fetched a makeshift stretcher while another opened a side door leading to a secluded infirmary. The convent's stone corridors were cool and quiet, the flickering light of Soeur Beatrice's candle that she carried before us giving it an air of timeless serenity. The faint scent of beeswax and incense lingered in the air, a subtle reminder of the prayers that had been offered here for centuries.

Denis and I carried Rook into the infirmary, the boy staggering under the weight but refusing to falter. The room was small but tidy, with rows of neatly folded linens and shelves lined with jars of herbs and rudimentary medical supplies. A simple crucifix hung on the wall above a narrow cot.

Sister Beatrice examined Rook with a practiced hand, her brow furrowing as she felt his pulse and checked his breathing. "He's gravely ill," she murmured, her voice steady but laced with concern. "We will do what we can, but..."

I nodded, understanding the unspoken reality. "Thank you," I said, my throat tight. "Please, just keep him comfortable."

As the sisters began their work, Denis sank into a wooden chair by the wall, his small frame slumped with exhaustion. I knelt beside him, placing a hand on his shoulder. "You were very brave, Denis. Your grandfather would be proud."

He looked at me with wide, tear-filled eyes. "Do you think he'll make it?" he whispered, his voice barely audible.

I hesitated, searching for the right words. "We've done all we can," I said finally. "Now it's in God's hands." I turned to Sister Beatrice. "You can care for this boy, too?"

"Of course." She motioned to one of the other sisters. "Give this brave young man a bite to eat and a bed to rest." To Denis, she said, "You have done your duty. Now you can rest." She made the sign of the cross over him.

Denis hadn't the energy to protest and followed the nun. He cast a look over his shoulder at me, and I waved. We both understood it was unlikely that we'd ever meet again.

Sister Beatrice glanced at me. "You also must be exhausted," she said gently. "There's a small room down the hall where you can rest."

I shook my head. "Not yet. I need to think."

She nodded her expression one of quiet sympathy. "You are safe here, mademoiselle. Take a moment to breathe."

As I stepped back into the courtyard, the cold night air wrapped around me like a shroud. The weight of the evening pressed heavily on my shoulders, and my mind raced with questions and doubts. Marianne's betrayal burned like a fresh wound, her actions replaying in my mind with cruel clarity. How had I missed the signs? Could I have stopped her? And why—why would she do this?

The stars above offered no answers, their distant light as unreachable as the world I longed to return to. Somehow, I had to get word of Marianne's duplicity to Captain Smithwick, but for now, all I could do was wait, pray, and hope that somewhere in the darkness, there was still a way forward.

As I stepped back into the convent, I was met by Sister Beatrice. "We have spoken to Denis. He's agreed to go to our brother monastery in the next town and stay there indefinitely, maybe even until the war is over. He can continue his schooling there with the brothers."

"Yes, it would be unsafe for him in the occupied territory now that the Germans know who he is and that he helped Rook escape. Please take care of him and shield him."

Sister Beatrice smiled and inclined her head. "Godspeed, mademoiselle."

Chapter Fifty-Two

REFLECTION AND ORDERS

October 20, 1916

THE TOWN OF BAR-LE-DUC, not far from the convent at Chaumont-sur-Aire, is a place that barely seems to breathe. The stone buildings lean together as if for comfort, their curtains drawn tightly against the outside world. The café where I was to meet Captain Smithwick was one of the few places showing signs of life. Smoke curled lazily from its chimney, and the faint clink of glasses sounded from within.

I entered quietly, my boots echoing on the worn wooden floor. Smithwick sat at a corner table, his uniform hidden beneath a civilian overcoat, a cup of steaming coffee before him. His expression was grim but softened slightly when he saw me.

"Ah, Mademoiselle LaFleur," he said, rising briefly before gesturing for me to sit.

I lowered myself into the chair opposite him, the weight of the past few days still pressing heavily on my shoulders. The warmth of the café was a sharp contrast to the chill outside, but it did little to thaw the cold knot in my chest.

"You look..." Smithwick hesitated, searching for the right word, "...tired."

"I am," I admitted, folding my hands on the table. "More than tired, really. I feel... hollow."

Smithwick nodded, his sharp blue eyes scanning my face. "After what you've been through, that's to be expected. I read your report. Marianne's betrayal, Rook... I can't imagine how you managed to get out of that alive."

"Barely," I said, my voice brittle. "And not without losses. Rook didn't survive the night. Marianne—" I paused, the name catching in my throat. "I trusted her, Smithwick. I trusted her with my life."

He sighed deeply, leaning back in his chair. "We've all had our share of betrayals in this line of work, but that doesn't make it any easier. Marianne's actions will be investigated, of course, but right now, our priority is you."

I blinked, caught off guard. "Me?"

"Yes," he said firmly. "Your cover is blown. Marianne knows your identity, your methods, and your contacts. She'll have already fed all of that to the Germans. It's no longer safe for you here."

My stomach tightened. Though I had anticipated this, hearing it said out loud made it real. "So what happens now?"

"You'll return to England," he said, his tone leaving no room for argument. "You need a reprieve—a chance to recover. And you'll receive a new identity before you're redeployed."

I opened my mouth to protest, but the words wouldn't come. Instead, I lowered my gaze to the table, tracing a knot in the wood with my finger. "I think... I think you're right," I said quietly.

Captain Smithwick's expression softened. "Good. I'm glad

you see that. Too often, agents push themselves past their breaking point, which never ends well."

I nodded, swallowing the lump in my throat. "Do you think Marianne... do you think she was always a double agent?"

Smithwick's brow furrowed as he considered the question. "It's hard to say. Double agents often start out loyal but are turned under pressure—threats, bribes, promises of safety for loved ones."

"She told the Germans exactly where to find us," I said, my voice tight. "She knew Rook's location, our safe house, our escape route. It wasn't just betrayal—it was precise, calculated."

Captain Smithwick leaned forward, resting his elbows on the table. "Let's think about her possible motives. What do we know about Marianne Chevalier?"

"She lived near Saint-Loup as a child—or so she claimed," I said. "She's fluent in German—more fluent than I realized. She once told me she worked for a German-speaking employer before the war, translating letters."

"That much I know as well. Perhaps her family has connections to the Germans," Captain Smithwick mused. "Or perhaps they're being held by the Boche. It's not uncommon for operatives to be turned when their families are threatened."

"Or bribed," I added bitterly. "The Germans have resources—money, promises of a better life. If Marianne thought the war was unwinnable, she might have decided to hedge her bets."

Captain Smithwick nodded, his expression grim. "It's also possible she was turned long ago, even before joining us. If that's the case, her entire time with the réseau has been a façade."

I clenched my fists, anger bubbling beneath the surface. "I don't want to believe that. But how can we ever know?"

"We may not," Captain Smithwick admitted. "But what matters now is that we act as though every piece of information she has is compromised. We'll change our codes, our routes, our contacts. And we'll learn from this."

Silence fell between us, the weight of the conversation settling like a thick fog. Finally, Captain Smithwick spoke again. "You did well. Better than anyone could have expected under the circumstances. Don't let Marianne Chevalier's actions define your work."

I nodded slowly, though his words offered little comfort. "When do I leave?"

"Tomorrow," he said. "A courier will meet you at dawn with papers and transport. You'll embark in Dieppe for England."

I stood, the chair scraping against the floor. "Thank you, Captain. For everything."

He rose as well, offering a faint smile. "Take care of yourself, Lady Gold. I will stay in contact."

As I stepped back into the cold streets of Bar-le-Duc, the night seemed darker than before. The wind bit at my skin, but I barely felt it. My thoughts were with Marianne, Rook, and the weight of the betrayal that had fractured our network, and a part of myself.

I departed the next day, and the following day I was on the ferry.

The sea was calmer than I had expected, though a persistent wind tore at my cloak and carried the acrid scent of salt and coal smoke through the damp air. The boat, a requisitioned steamer half-full of returning officers, nurses, and a handful of civilians, rocked gently as it cut through the waves. I stood near the railing, gripping it tightly as the French coastline faded into the mist behind us.

England lay ahead.

I exhaled, pressing a gloved hand against my forehead. How long would I have to stay? Ambrosia had been made aware of my return to Bray Manor, and though I knew she would welcome me, a part of me chafed at the thought of being away from my work. From France.

Will it be weeks? Months? Is it possible I'll be forbidden to return?

I glanced toward the deck where two officers stood talking in low voices, their khaki coats buttoned high against the October chill. Their faces were drawn, their shoulders heavy with the same exhaustion I had seen in too many men these past months. How long will this accursed war last? The newspapers in France spoke of heavy losses on the Somme, of mud, blood, and a battle that seems to stretch on without end.

A gust of wind caught my hat, nearly pulling it from my head, and I clamped a hand over it just in time. If I do return to France, what will I be returning to? The hospitals are full, the supply lines strained, and each day brings fresh reports of casualties.

Daniel is still there.

My chest tightened.

If only I could convince Captain Smithwick to arrange a meeting—even a brief one—if I could just see him for a moment, my heart would overflow. Unfortunately, the army doesn't grant favors for the sake of sentiment.

I pulled my cloak more tightly around me, the cold seeping through my woolen dress. Somewhere behind me, a soldier coughed—a deep, ragged sound that carried across the deck. I turned slightly, glancing at the others aboard. The nurses sat huddled together, talking quietly, their faces pale with exhaustion. A young boy, no older than sixteen, stood near the lifeboats, staring toward England with a clenched jaw and haunted eyes. Too young to be a soldier, but in this war, what did that matter?

The steamer pressed forward, carrying me back to England, back to Ambrosia, back to a world that seemed both familiar and foreign after so much time away.

The truth is, I don't know how long I will stay, nor what awaits me when I return to the continent.

All I knew was that I had to go back to France.

Back to the work that matters.

Back to him.

If you enjoyed reading *The Velvet Spy ~ Volume 1* please help others enjoy it too.

Recommend it: Help others find the book by recommending it to friends, readers' groups, discussion boards and by **suggesting it to your local library.**

Review it: Please tell other readers why you liked this book by reviewing it on at your point of purchase or Goodreads.

* No spoilers please *

Don't miss
THE VELVET SPY ~ VOLUME 2
THE WARTIME JOURNAL OF LADY GOLD

HISTORY REMEMBERS THE BATTLES. Her journal remembers the cost.

Lady Ginger Gold returns to the heart of the Great War—where danger deepens, trust is scarce, and the cost of courage grows ever higher.

In this gripping conclusion of her secret wartime journal, Ginger faces increasingly perilous missions across occupied Europe. But it's not only enemy lines she must navigate—her own heart bears the weight of devastating personal loss.

As the stakes rise and the shadows close in, The Velvet Spy reveals the true cost of sacrifice—and the unbreakable spirit of a woman who refuses to give in.

leestraussbooks.com

About the Author

Lee Strauss is a Canadian USA TODAY bestselling author of The Ginger Gold Mysteries series, The Higgins & Hawke Mystery series, The Rosa Reed Mystery series (cozy historical mysteries), A Nursery Rhyme Mystery series (mystery suspense), The Light & Love series (sweet romance), The Clockwise Collection (YA time travel romance), and young adult historical fiction with over a million books read. She has titles published in German and French, and a growing audio library.

When Lee's not writing or reading she likes to cycle, hike, and stare at the ocean. She loves to drink caffè lattes and red wines in exotic places, and eat dark chocolate anywhere.

For more info on books by Lee Strauss and her social media links, visit leestraussbooks.com. To make sure you don't miss the next new release, be sure to sign up for her readers' list!

Discuss the books, ask questions, share your opinions. Fun giveaways! Join the Lee Strauss Readers' Group on Facebook for more info.

Did you know you can follow your favourite authors on Bookbub? If you subscribe to Bookbub — (and if you don't, why don't you? - They'll send you daily emails alerting you to sales and new releases on just the kind of books you like to read!) — follow me to make sure you don't miss the next Ginger Gold Mystery!

Find me on Pinterest

www.leestraussbooks.com
leestraussbooks@gmail.com

More from Lee Strauss

The Velvet Spy ~ The Wartime Journal of Ginger Gold

Volume 1

Volume 2

GINGER GOLD MYSTERY SERIES (cozy 1920s historical)

Cozy. Charming. Filled with Bright Young Things. This Jazz Age murder mystery will entertain and delight you with its 1920s flair and pizzazz!

Murder on the SS Rosa

Murder at Hartigan House

Murder at Bray Manor

Murder at Feathers & Flair

Murder at the Mortuary

Murder at Kensington Gardens

Murder at St. George's Church

The Wedding of Ginger & Basil

Murder Aboard the Flying Scotsman

Murder at the Boat Club

Murder on Eaton Square

Murder by Plum Pudding

Murder on Fleet Street

Murder at Brighton Beach

Murder in Hyde Park

Murder at the Royal Albert Hall

Murder in Belgravia

Murder on Mallowan Court

Murder at the Savoy

Murder at the Circus

Murder in France

Murder at Yuletide

Murder at Madame Tussauds

Murder at St. Paul's Cathedral

Murder at the Olympics

Murder at the Cave of Harmony

LADY GOLD INVESTIGATES (Ginger Gold companion short stories)

Volume 1

Volume 2

Volume 3

Volume 4

Volume 5

Volume 6

HIGGINS & HAWKE MYSTERY SERIES (cozy 1930s historical)

The 1930s meets Rizzoli & Isles in this friendship depression era cozy mystery series.

Death at the Tavern

Death on the Tower

Death on Hanover

Death by Dancing

Death on Tremont Row

Death at King's Chapel

THE ROSA REED MYSTERIES

(1950s cozy historical)

Murder at High Tide

Murder on the Boardwalk

Murder at the Bomb Shelter

Murder on Location

Murder and Rock 'n Roll

Murder at the Races

Murder at the Dude Ranch

Murder in London

Murder at the Fiesta

Murder at the Weddings

A NURSERY RHYME MYSTERY SERIES(mystery/sci fi)

Marlow finds himself teamed up with intelligent and savvy Sage Farrell, a girl so far out of his league he feels blinded in her presence - literally - damned glasses! Together they work to find the identity of @gingerbreadman. Can they stop the killer before he strikes again?

Gingerbread Man

Life Is but a Dream

Hickory Dickory Dock

Twinkle Little Star

LIGHT & LOVE (sweet romance)

Set in the dazzling charm of Europe, follow Katja, Gabriella, Eva, Anna and Belle as they find strength, hope and love.

Love Song

Your Love is Sweet

In Light of Us

Lying in Starlight

PLAYING WITH MATCHES (WW2 history/romance)

A sobering but hopeful journey about how one young German boy copes with the war and propaganda. Based on true events.

A Piece of Blue String (companion short story)

THE CLOCKWISE COLLECTION (YA time travel romance)

Casey Donovan has issues: hair, height and uncontrollable trips to the 19th century! And now this ~ she's accidentally taken Nate Mackenzie, the cutest boy in the school, back in time. Awkward.

Clockwise

Clockwiser

Like Clockwork

Counter Clockwise

Clockwork Crazy

Clocked (companion novella)

Standalones

Seaweed

Love, Tink

www.ingramcontent.com/pod-product-compliance
Lightning Source LLC
Chambersburg PA
CBHW020358210626
46816CB00006BB/2021